MESMERIZED

Garnet Wells

Mesmerized by Garnet Wells

Copyright © 2019 by Hustle & Write Publishing, LLC

Cover design by Amber G. Hustle & Write Publishing, LLC

Editing – Reflected Gifts

Editing – Amber D. Walls

Compiled by – Amber G.

ISBN-13: 978-1-7321516-3-5
Printed in the United States of America.

For information regarding the other releases under Hustle & Write Publishing please visit www.hustleandwritepublishing.com or connect with us on the following social media websites:

Facebook – books by Amber G

Instagram – @booksbyAmberG

DEDICATION

Even though I'm no longer here, may my legacy live on in these words. Thanks to all of you who made my first book a possibility.

Garnet Wells

May 27, 1953 – June 7, 2018

There is life after death, and it's beautiful. It's a place where happiness abides and all are healed and united.

MESMERIZED

Chapter One

Kosby

I parked my brand-new Cadillac sedan in the parking space allotted to me when I closed on my new condo. I was eager to see my new place. I walked over to the elevator and stepped inside. I pushed my floor and right as the door started to close, this guy stuck his foot in, and the doors reopened. He pushed his floor, and politely said,

"Hello."

I was surprised to see a brother living in this building. I don't know why because we are indeed successful in all walks of life.

"Hi," I responded as I turned my head back to the front of the elevator. I glanced at him, and he was looking at me, so I smiled. He was a good-looking brother, about six-foot-four. He had beautiful deep bronze skin that accentuated his jet-black wavy hair. The sides and back were freshly cut into a fade. He had a five o'clock shadow, with a thicker mustache completing the connection. His eyes were so beautiful. I found myself staring.

"What color are your eyes?"

He laughed, "Blue."

"I know they are blue, but the color is such a unique mixture of royal and navy. I've never seen eyes that color. And your lashes are luxurious." He let out a hearty laugh. "I don't understand why men have lashes women would fight for."

Just before we reached my floor, the elevator jiggled and stopped. He pushed a red button, and an alarm went off. The alarm was silenced, and security said,"

"Ms. Matthews, Mr. Richards, we'll have the elevator running in a moment."

Mr. Richards replied, "Take your time. Being stuck in this elevator with this gorgeous woman has been the highlight of my day." I blushed.

"Does this happen a lot?" I asked, growing concerned.

"No, they usually are very reliable. I'd be at home now if I waited for the next elevator, but I had to catch a glimpse of the beautiful woman I saw inside this one."

"You mean me?"

"Yes, you," he whispered. "You're very attractive."

The elevator began to move. I stopped it before reaching my floor.

"Thank you," I mumbled, hitting the stop button. I reached in my purse and grabbed my iPhone. I stood next to him, told him to smile, and took a quick selfie of us. I hit the button once again. Before he could ask, I stepped out of the elevator. I heard it take off as I walked to my unit.

I used my key to open the door, after which I shut and locked it. I was excited to see my place alone before my girl, Kiarra arrived. I was even more interested in looking at the photo I just snapped. It was gorgeous; a good shot of me, but he was so handsome. Those eyes had me mesmerized. I never picked the good-looking guys. I always fell for the intellect. I put my phone down and walked to the front window. I stood there, admiring the view of the strip.

"So, what do you think?" I asked Kiarra with a big smile on my face as we walked around my very first home purchase.

"You know I love it, Kosby. Your place is awesome. These floor to ceiling windows are gorgeous, and dang, how tall are these ceilings?"

I smiled. "Ten-foot ceilings, open floor plan with designer stone flooring, Bosch stainless steel appliances, and Italian cabinets."

"Wow," Kiarra replied. "I am so jealous. You can see the Las Vegas strip from your front window. You're in the heart of City Center with great shopping, dining, and entertainment."

"Yep, now you can help me with the furniture shopping," I said as I grabbed my purse and keys off the granite countertop. Kiarra and Stacey were my best friends. We bonded in grade school and never split up. Stacey was an obstetrician and couldn't make our little shopping spree because she was delivering a baby.

We searched a lot of furniture stores, but I didn't find what I had in mind. Not wanting to make a hasty decision and regret it later, I suggested we stop at this cute little bistro and have a bite to eat. Kiarra concurred. We sat down, ready to get our grub on. I ordered the jerk chicken salad while Kiarra had a Cobb salad. We had a ball talking.

"So, I met a man. He's a Las Vegas policeman. Girl, he's very well-mannered." Kiarra's eyes smiled when she talked about how they were enjoying getting to know each other.

"Do you think it would be okay if I brought him to your father's retirement party on Saturday?"

"We would love to meet him. Stacey's coming with Carl."

"Good," Kiarra chimed. "She married well. I wonder what it's like to be a power couple making megabucks?"

"I know, right! They have that beautiful estate in the mountains."

"I wonder if they ever get to see it together?" I joked.

We both laughed. "They probably have

squatters in the west wing," Kiarra said as we continued to laugh.

"My entire two-bedroom condo is the size of her walk-in closet."

We looked at each other, and another wave of laughter erupted. After we calmed down, Kiarra said, "You know we can joke about each other, but no one else can."

"I know that's right. We stuck together through grade school, middle school, and high school. Heck, we stayed besties attending different colleges and universities."

The next day I woke up feeling rested and excited. I wasn't on my routine this morning. Most Sundays, I spent getting ready for church. I grew up in the church. I was a Junior Usher, and I sang with the Children's Choir. I never lost my roots. But now, my excitement about my new condo was overwhelming. So ready to move in, I had to find some furniture and shopping yesterday with Kiarra had been a bust. I said a little prayer and asked God to forgive me for not attending church and to give me his divine blessing on finding the perfect furniture for my new place.

I drove over to an industrial area that featured a lot of businesses that sold goods for homes. Some of them only open to commercial builders, others were open to the public.

I envisioned buying a white, taupe or wheat colored sectional, but my eyes went straight to a gray sectional that was so beautiful I could only stand there and look at it.

I searched for a salesperson and found a nice older lady who made me feel very comfortable. I showed her the items that caught my eye.

"I have to have them all," I chuckled.

"They are beautiful. I see why you love them so much. We also have the cocktail table and the end tables that match. Would you like to look at them?"

"Sure," I responded. As we walked over to another area in the showroom, I could see they were a perfect match, simple yet elegant.

"I love everything! Where are the prices? I inquired.

"We work a little different than most stores. The more you buy from us, the better price you get. Are you interested in anything else?"

"Yeah, I need a bedroom set."

She smiled at me. "Come this way. We have lots of bedroom furniture," she replied.

Chapter Two

Kiarra

I tried to relax in the tub. I got the water as hot as I could stand it and threw in my Thousand Wishes bath bomb. I watched the fireworks spin and twirl. It smelled so good. I had a date later with one of Las Vegas' finest police officers. Mmhmm honey, let me tell you about Officer Derrick Andrews.

I met Derrick on Labor Day. I was on my way to my cousins' cookout. I had just parked my car when I saw a vehicle barreling down the residential street, going at least 60 miles per hour, maybe even faster. The vehicle got to the busy corner and made it across without incident. A six-foot stone wall was at the end of the road, and unfortunately, the car hit that wall. I watched. It seemed surreal. The wall went tumbling down on the vehicle. Within seconds, the car was buried in debris. Three women started running down the street, screaming and saying words that didn't register with me. As I got to the passenger's side of my car to grab the potato salad. I could hear a woman yell,

"Does anyone have a crowbar?" I didn't know what she thought she could do with a crowbar because whoever was in that car had gone to meet their maker.

I walked into my cousin's house and headed out back where the family greeted me. I told them about the accident outside, and several people went to look. I grabbed an ice-cold bottle of water and sat down under a tree. I prayed for whoever was in that car. I had to let it go for my peace of mind. That was hard to do with the melody of sirens in the air. My cousin Sherri walked over to me. I stood up, and we hugged. We both sat down.

"You are rocking that dress, Kiarra, but you always were a beauty inside and out."

"Thank you, Sherri. I feel the same way about you."

"Did you bring the potato salad?" Sherri inquired.

"Yes, I did. It's in the refrigerator awaiting mealtime."

Before we could make more small talk, I heard my cousin Kenny calling my name. I waved at him, and he walked over.

"There is a police officer on the front porch who wants to talk to you."

"Thanks, Kenny," I said as I got up and walked toward the porch, wondering what this man could want with me.

Shut the front door! I did not expect Officer Goody to be tall, dark chocolate, and FINE! I took a deep breath because I hadn't seen a fine, knockout gorgeous brother in a while. *I hope he isn't married*; I thought to myself.

Trying to remain calm, and collected, I said,

"I'm Kiarra, did you want to speak to me?"

"Yes," he responded. "I'm Officer Andrews. I was told you witnessed the accident up the street."

"Yes, I had just gotten out of my car when I saw this vehicle going down the street at a high rate of speed. The car went straight through traffic at the corner and barreled into that high wall."

"How do you spell Kiarra," he asked in his official voice.

I spelled it for him and told him my last name.

"Is this your address," he asked. I told him no and gave him my address and phone number. He then said, "House or cell phone number?"

I deliberately didn't answer. I waited for the officer to look at me. I rolled my eyes and twisted my head in disdain. He changed his stance.

"Just give it to the detective. He should be able to figure that one out!" I said, being sassy.

He smiled at me. "I wasn't asking for the detective." He commented in his deepest baritone.

I remembered thinking what a creative

way for him to ask for my number.

I ran some more hot water into my cooling bath; I laid back on the bath pillow, not quite ready to get out. I was proud of my accomplishments despite my upbringing. Stacey and Kosby had parents with good jobs. I came from a single-family home with six brothers and two sisters. We lived in Section Eight Housing, and because of food stamps, we ate at least half of the month.

In high school, Kosby and I both made the cheerleading squad. I was going to quit because my mother couldn't afford to buy my uniform. Kosby's parents paid for my uniform. They were so nice. I'm blessed to have them as friends.

Stacey never noticed men flirting with her or looking at her. She was the only one married. She and her husband fell in love as residents. Kosby, on the other hand, was a perfectionist. I'm sure that, and her natural ability with math got her where she is today. Heck, I had never even heard of an Actuary until Kosby became one. I'm sure graduating with honors from Purdue University in Mathematics didn't hurt either. I have always envied Kosby, not her math ability, but her looks. She could have been a model or a movie star. She was stunning yet modest. She lived with her parents after graduation, worked hard, and saved most of her money. So, I'm not surprised Kosby purchased that gorgeous condo in the heart of the city, with a bird's-eye view of the strip. She was so humble, not mentioning her two-bedroom condo cost almost as much as Stacey's massive estate in the mountains.

I rent my apartment, but I'm not having a pity party. I started working while they both went to universities. I started as a clerk, and through hard work, I became an administrative assistant.

After my bath, it didn't take me long to put on my makeup and get dressed. I was done in a jiffy, eagerly awaiting Derrick's arrival. The doorbell rang. I looked at the clock, and he was right on time. Yes! That's what I'm talking about, a man who doesn't take you for granted. I opened the door. He was so handsome and thoughtful as he handed me a vase of beautiful flowers.

"Thank you," I told him as I walked over to the dining table to set them down, making sure they were in the perfect spot. This was our third date. Just looking at him made my body tingle.

We went to the Eiffel Tower for dinner. I was excited because even though I lived in Vegas, I had never eaten there. Seated promptly at a table by the window, the view of the Bellagio was magnificent. It was awesome watching their water show. The atmosphere was decent but very conservative. Everything was monotone with the tables dressed in white linen, with white candles and white flowers. He caressed my hand as we enjoyed the ambiance of the evening.

The attraction I felt with this man was electric. It delighted me. I prayed he was the right man for me.

Chapter Three

Kosby

I paced the floor, barefoot on the cold stone. Today was the big day, my dad's retirement party. I made sure I had taken care of everything, so there would be no hiccups at my dad's big event. I reserved a ballroom with seating for two hundred guests, with a DJ and dance floor. My boss let me use the ballroom free of charge. He said we had an outstanding year and my calculations had been right on point. My brother Chris surprised us when he got one of the hottest DJ's in the city to do the affair. I glanced at the clock — time for me to get to the venue. Carlos, one of the guys that did decorations for Caesars, promised to blow up balloons if I met him there at eight a.m.

Dressed in a t-shirt and jeans, I was ready to work. I threw on a pair of flats and hightailed it to the ballroom.

"Thank you, Carlos."

"You're welcome, Kosby. I have a big surprise for you."

"What is it?" I inquired, like a kid on Christmas. "I'll show you as soon as we get the balloons blown up," Carlos answered.

We placed bouquets of balloons around the room to create a festive display. Carlos looked at his watch.

"8:35," he murmured as he put the helium back on the dolly.

"I'll be back in a couple of minutes with your surprise."

I still had a happy retirement banner with my dad's airline insignia to hang. Carlos came back in the room, rolling a table with vases of red roses and a large centerpiece for the main table. My mouth flung open.

"Wow, Carlos," I screamed as I jumped for joy.

"I'll be back later to get the table. When your guests leave tonight, make sure they do not take the vases."

"Got it, my friend, I think I can handle that." I retorted slipping twenty dollars in his hand. I hung the banner and placed the vases on the center of each table. My friends were all coming with dates. I was the only one without one.

Later that evening, the first to arrive, I turned on the lights. Before I could do anything else, David arrived with a table full of candles.

"Hi Kosby," he blurted out. "You look absolutely stunning."

"Thank you, David, are you working at my party tonight?"

"Yes, I am. Aren't these candles lovely, we

just got these in stock."

"They sure are." I smiled.

Things began to move fast. Workers set up a bar in the corner equipped with shelves. There was alcohol, a variety of mixes and garnishes — and a refrigerator filled with various beers and wine, along with an ice chest with soda and water. In came a portable shelf filled with glassware of all kinds, and the bartender stocked his station with red and blue napkins. The caterers rolled in carts with hors d' oeuvres to soothe every palate. DJ Phire was all set up at the DJ station and played his first tune of the evening, some soothing jazz. I walked over to the DJ booth and introduced myself,

"Would you like something to drink?"

"Yes, a beer would be nice."

"Any special brand," I inquired.

"A Bud Light if they have it."

I got a Bud Light from the bartender and took it to the DJ booth. I greeted friends and my father's work associates. I sat with my mother, who was at the table all alone.

"Having fun, mom?"

"Yes, look at your dad, the center of attention. I'm afraid he'll miss that in retirement."

"No, mommy, I don't think so. He knows everyone in the neighborhood, and he loves to golf. It'll be just like it was on his days off, but every day."

We both giggled. Chris came and sat down with his girlfriend, Sheila. I glanced at my dad. His group was even larger. That's when I saw Mr. Richards from the elevator. Unbelievable, I never saw him again in my building, but here he was at my father's retirement party. My palms began to sweat. I wondered if I should go talk to him. No, he could have found me if he were interested. Plus, once we were seated, I could see who he brought to this soiree.

"Kosby, Kosby," I heard my brother say.

"Huh," I responded as I joined the conversation.

"Would you like another drink? I'm going to the bar."

"No, thank you, Chris, I'm still nursing my first one." I saw Stacey and Carl come in. I grabbed my drink to join them at their table when I noticed Kiarra and Derrick already seated. I sat down and spoke to everyone, trying my best to keep my cool and be cordial.

"Now, this is a nice retirement party," said Carl.

"Thank you," I answered, knowing he was used to the finer things in life.

"This is my date, Derrick," Kiarra said.
I shook his hand. "Nice to meet you. I've heard so many wonderful things about you."

He smiled. "Same here. Kiarra loves her friends, so I feel like I already know you all."

We all made introductions for Derrick. I

sat and smiled at my friends as they made several comments. All I heard was mumbo jumbo though because I kept glancing at Mr. Richards; a man I dreamt about, yet I didn't even know his first name. The group kept up the chit chat as I nervously rubbed my perspiring hands under the table. Again, I heard my name. I snapped back, wondering what I had missed. My first-time meeting Derrick, and he probably thought I rode the short bus.

"That's ok, Kosby," Carl said. "This is your dad's big night."

I smiled. What a gentleman he was letting me off the hook. My friends continued to talk. I stood up, making an excuse to leave the group, promising to return later. As I walked away from the table, I could hear my father yell my name. I looked at him, gave him my I love you Daddy smile as I headed in his direction.

"Gentleman, this is my princess, my baby girl, Kosby."

I smiled, and in my sweet voice said, "Hi everybody."

I heard a bunch of hi's, hey's, and hellos. I looked at Mr. Richards and said, "It's good to see you again."

My dad asked. "Do you know this young man?"

"Not really, dad. I got stuck on an elevator with him for about two minutes when I first moved into my condo."

My dad asked Mr. Richards, "Why didn't you tell me you met my daughter?"

"I didn't know I met your daughter. Matter of fact, I just learned her first name when you said, let me introduce my daughter." He grabbed his napkin from under his drink and dabbed the perspiration from his forehead.

All the men laughed and continued their conversations. I turned to walk away. He came after me.

"Kosby!" I turned around, drawn to those piercing eyes.

"I'm sorry if I was rude. My name is Deion Richards. I'm a pilot at the same airlines your father works for. He trained me as a co-pilot, and he's a great guy. I should have known he would have a stunning daughter."

Yeah right, "That's why you tried so hard to find me; you had more clues than Prince Charming in Cinderella. You knew what floor I lived on, you knew my last name, and because of the selfie, you knew I was interested. But you blew me off, never giving me a second thought." I tried to walk away.

He raced for me. "No, it wasn't like that. I knew your floor, but what was I supposed to do, knock on every door and ask, does Ms. Matthews live here? I looked for you in my own way. I stood in the parking garage at about the same time of day. That didn't work. I wished I saw you get out of your car. But I didn't have a clue what car you drove without feeling like a stalker." We both laughed.

"This is a beautiful party for your dad."

"Thanks, it's only just begun. Don't run away before dinner."

"You're not getting rid of me that fast. Before I leave tonight, I will have the apartment number, the telephone number, be a Facebook friend, Instagram, Twitter, and Snapchat!"

"You are hilarious," I giggled.

"No, I've been given a second chance, and believe me, I won't blow it. Would you like another drink?" he asked.

"Sure, and I'm buying!"

Again, we both laughed because I was paying for the open bar. "So, do you enjoy flying planes?"

"Yes, I love it. I feel so blessed to have such a wonderful job. Your father has been my mentor. I will miss working with him."

"Do you play golf?" I asked.

"Yes, I love the game."

"Well, my dad loves to play, so you'll have a new best friend."

"I've golfed with your dad plenty of times. I remember he showed me a picture of you as a cheerleader."

I almost choked, "No, he didn't show you that." I rolled my eyes, "That was a whole lot of years ago. My friend Kiarra was on the team with me; ha-ha she was also in that old picture."

I pointed in her direction.

"You were the cutest cheerleader on the team, but I didn't make the connection that you were the beauty in the elevator."

"Where are you sitting," I inquired.

"At the men's table, you know all the men who RSVP'd with no plus one." he laughed.

"That just increased your cool points. I'll have you moved to my table."

"Is your dad going to be sitting at the table?"

"Yes."

"No, I'll pass. Your dad is super protective of you. I must come to you right, so I don't upset your father."

"Of course," I responded, *unsure how to take that. Humph, only time would tell.*

"It's nice to know your name, Deion. I'm going to sit with my mother. She's alone," I said warmly.

"I'll go over there with you because I want your phone number, that is if you want to share it with me."

"I would like that." I led him to our table and introduced him to my mother. They held a conversation with ease, so I calmed down and let the evening flow. We exchanged phone numbers and apartment numbers. It felt like a good day to me. I had thought of this man every day since I first laid eyes on him. We were hitting it off, but I knew that it could go south, too. I was a realist, and usually, if it was too good to be true, it probably was.

The DJ announced it was mealtime and asked everyone to return to their assigned seats. I had my iPhone in my hand from exchanging phone numbers with Deion. I pushed the camera and asked my mom to take a photo of us. She agreed. I stood up, and so did he. To my surprise, he put his arm around my shoulder, and we posed as mom took about ten pictures. I hated watching Deion go, but there was still partying to be had after dinner.

He walked away just as my dad was returning. Dad was smiling ear to ear, so I knew he was having an enjoyable time. My brother returned with Sheila, and they continued whatever conversation they were having. My dad entertained mom and me with his stories about his friends. He could spin a fascinating tale. We just never knew how much was embellished. But it didn't matter because it made him feel important.

The food was delicious. I walked down to the kitchen; I saw the Chef busy giving out orders. I waited patiently because this man was working his magic. When he finished, I walked over, introduced myself, and asked him if he catered my party.

He said, "yes," with concern.

"The food, the service; everything was magnificent," I told him.

He smiled and hugged me. I grabbed his hand and thanked him.

I hadn't expected that, but it's always good to compliment someone who did an exceptional job. While I was away, this event had turned into a party. Folks were laughing, people were dancing on the ballroom floor, and DJ Phire, was off the chain. I walked over to the dance floor and joined in. Before I knew it, Deion was by my side, and the DJ was not letting up with a floor full of folks dancing. After we had done every version of this same dance DJ Phire slowed the music down and put on a slow jam. Deion grabbed my arm, and I looked up at those captivating eyes. My mind was saying yes, but these high heels I had on were saying *naw girl this ain't going to work.*

"Sorry, Deion, my feet are screaming in these heels."

"Let's sit down," he suggested, and he pointed to some cute leather benches by the wall.

"Wow, you know how to throw a party," Deion remarked.

"It was a lot of fun; my dad is the best. Even with his crazy work schedule, he had a lot of time to spend with the family. He seemed to enjoy every recital, every game, and every play he could make. I never resented it when he couldn't come because of work. I knew he would be there if he could."

"Your father is so blessed. You have a great family. My dad couldn't hold a job. He was mean and had a stroke at 36 years old."

"Wow, I'm so sorry. That must have been difficult for you. Both my best friends are from single-parent homes, so I shared my dad with them. They call him dad, too."

"He often mentioned his adopted daughters. I thought they lived with you." Deion said.

"We were always at each other's houses, but we all had our own homes. I'll introduce them to you as soon as my pinkie toe stops hurting." I laughed.

"Would you like a drink?" he asked.

"Yes, I answered, a margarita blended no ice and salt on the rim."

"Got it. I'll be back in a moment."

He was back in a jiffy and handed me the drink, then sat next to me and drank his Martini.

"So, did you meet your friends in school?"

"Yes, we did. Vegas doesn't have a good school system, but my mother, who still works as a teacher, would give us lessons after school. We hated it, but it paid off because Stacey is an obstetrician and Kiarra, an administrative assistant."

"Ok, you know I'm a pilot; what do you do?"

"I'm an Actuary right here at Caesars

Palace."

"So, you are good with numbers?" he inquired.

"Yes, I'm good with numbers. I enjoy my job. Come on; I'll introduce you to my girls because I see they are both in their seats."

We walked over to their table. I introduced everyone that I knew. We sat in an empty setting at their table; we all began to have conversations. It was hilarious because I had never talked about Deion, so they had a zillion question for him.

"Did you two meet tonight?" Kiarra asked.

Crazy looks passed between them when they found out we lived in the same building. Their jaw dropped when they found out Deion was a pilot and flew with dad. It was so much fun. Everyone seemed to be having a great time! We all knew we had a lot to talk about on the next phone conversation. Derrick asked if anyone wanted a drink, everyone declined.

"I hope everyone is taking Uber or Lyft home, or someone who didn't drink is the designated driver?" I questioned.

Stacey said, "Kosby, you and Deion could walk home."

"Not in these shoes, I can't. I'd be lucky to make it to the car."

Everyone giggled, now the jokes were rampant among the group. Carl told Stacey,

"You should walk home. You're getting a

little chunky."

The entire group grew quiet.

"Don't talk about a sister's weight. Those are fighting words," Kiarra chimed in.

I looked into Deion's dreamy eyes. We got caught up in a staring contest. Derrick came back, and the jokes started rolling again, we were having a great time.

They wheeled in the cake. It had sparklers around the edges. All you could hear were the ooh, and aah's from everyone.

"It's time to cut the cake." Blurted DJ Phire.

They sat the cake in its designated area. We all got up and went by the table as my dad said his parting words to his old airline. My mom got teary-eyed, so I walked over to her and dabbed her face so she wouldn't ruin her make-up. They opened the champagne bottles and gave a glass to the family and then to anyone else who wanted a glass.

DJ Phire slowed the rhythm down. Everyone began to slow dance.

"Want to dance," Deion asked.

"Yes, I do."

On the dance floor, my head felt comfortable on his shoulder. Not sure if it was his slender but muscular physique, his cologne, his beautiful skin color or maybe all of it coupled with those hypnotic eyes, but I was mesmerized. I never felt like this about a man. Oh, I liked plenty of men, but Deion was different. I didn't want to fall for him. Most men started out nice until you realized they were jerks. Wasn't hard for me to say goodbye because I fell in love with men's minds. The more intelligent they were, the more I liked them. He surprised me being a pilot. That took intelligence and a lot of training to transport people safely from one place to another.

He acted like I was his woman. The only other cute guy I ever dated did the same thing. We stayed together for over a year, which was a long time at that age. He found someone he felt was cuter, lighter skin, and her parents were well off. No, I wanted no more of that superficial bull crap. Just thinking about how he broke up with me, people laughed at me. I had to learn to be strong! Acted like I didn't care, turned my head when I saw them walking together. I didn't date for a long time, threw myself into my studies, so I thanked him for that. *Deion, if I take a big leap of faith in trusting you, please don't let me fall.*

My dad's party was over, and I was glad to call it a night. I took off my heels, put them in my bag, and threw on my flats. Everyone left except me, the workers, and DJ Phire. I had someone coming to help him load his gear. I took down the decorations, kept the banner, and gave the balloons away. I loaded the rose vases on a table so Carlos could pick them up in the morning. I called housecleaning to clean the tables and vacuum the floor. To my surprise, Carlos was on duty; he was happy I had loaded the vases, and they were all there. I grabbed my bag, got in the elevator, and walked to my car.

I drove the short distance home parked and went up to my apartment. It didn't take me long to put on my nightgown, wash my face, and wrap my hair in a satin scarf. I do believe I was asleep before my head hit the pillow.

Chapter Four

Deion

I glanced at the clock. It was almost 1 p.m. I was just now waking up. Groggy with a headache, I grabbed two Excedrin from the medicine cabinet and headed to the kitchen, where I poured myself a glass of orange juice. I drank too much. I'm going back to my two-drink rule... jeez. Blessed, I got home okay without hitting something or worse, someone. I would have put my job in jeopardy had I gotten a DUI.

In the shower, I let the hot water run down my head to my toes. It felt so good. I enjoyed yesterday. Funny how God opens doors even when you think they're shut. I'll never forget the day I first saw her beautiful chocolate complexion with a full head of natural hair. I loved natural hair on a sister, so I sped up to get on the elevator with her. The doors were closing. I stuck my foot in front of the elevator in time to reopen the door. She stood there; her features so beautiful, I knew she was a queen. She glanced at me as I stepped inside the elevator. To my surprise, she gave a stunning smile. Just as I was ready to rap to her, the elevator rattled and stopped. I could tell she was shaken.

"Does this happen often?" she asked.

I told her, "no."

I hit the alarm to let the security know we were stuck on the elevator. They told us they'd have it up and running momentarily. When security spoke over the intercom, I took a mental note that they called her Ms. Matthew's. I was disappointed I'd lost contact with her. I felt like she was attracted to me, too. Otherwise, I had no explanation of why she grabbed her phone and took a selfie of us before exiting the elevator. I admit I had to laugh once the elevator doors shut.

The best thing was daydreaming about a woman you met, but you couldn't ever seem to find again. So, meeting her again yesterday at Mr. Matthews retirement party was indeed a dream come true. She was stunning. Everyone was dressed in after five attire, but she took it to another level wearing a beautiful red pants suit. Her perfume was captivating, her jewelry bold. She had on a bracelet reminiscent of something Wonder Woman would wear. I found out her name was Kosby. What an intriguing name for such a beautiful woman. I thought I was in heaven. It isn't every day that you meet the woman of your dreams. Her voice was melodic, laugh alluring. I followed her around the party like a puppy follows his master. I prayed I didn't mess up by doing something dumb like spilling my food or drink.

I'd follow up that fantastic night with a bouquet. I wasn't even sure which flowers would be appropriate, but I'm sure the florist would recommend something. Yeah, that's what I'd do, she might even think I had a little class. It was refreshing to meet an intelligent young lady with a career she enjoyed. She wasn't looking for someone to be her meal ticket. Kosby was so amazing to me. She could be the one! One look at her, and I was mesmerized.

My head was feeling better, but I was still dragging. Guess I'd get up and go to the gym. After the workout, I dragged myself back to my condo. I got back in the shower this time to cleanse my body of the alcohol I sweat out after all that drinking from last night.

I called the florist and ordered Kosby flowers. The florist suggested a colorful bouquet of carnations. He said they say I "like" you, but this was just a first date. The card read nice meeting you, again and my name. I turned on some music, got out my cleaning supplies, and started to get my cleaning done.

I always liked the way the house smelled after a good cleaning. I was singing and dancing to the music because I was happy about the new lady I hoped to keep in my life. I ordered takeout Chinese food, turned on the TV, sat down to take a break, as I waited for the delivery.

I headed to bed. I had an early morning flight. We had a lot of stops to make with the last stop in Miami, Florida. We would end our destination in Las Vegas, and then have a day off. With a couple of days behind me, it would be an appropriate time for me to call Kosby.

I couldn't even get my clothes off before I dialed her number. I was so happy to talk to her. We texted a few times, and she thanked me for the flowers, but this was the first time we talked since the night of the party. She told me about her day, and I told her about mine. We decided we both missed each other and were looking forward to an official date.

Chapter Five

Kosby

I sat on my stainless-steel bar stool while I ate a healthy dinner, broiled chicken, asparagus, and a nice Caesar salad. I couldn't help but think about Deion. Lately, he was always on my mind. I was thrilled when I received the gorgeous bouquet of carnations in a beautiful array of colors. He was working, so I didn't call him to thank him, but I sent him a text I knew he would read when he had time.

I had so much fun talking to Kiarra.

"Oh, you've been holding out on me. You didn't tell me you met that cutie in the elevator in your building."

I laughed. "I know. I didn't know if I'd ever see that man again. To be honest, I hadn't seen him until my dad's retirement party. Girl, my heart was palpitating, my hands were perspiring and clammy; it was a trip." We both giggled.

"What did you think when you saw him," she asked.

"I thought I was in the Twilight Zone; I started looking around for Rod Serling."

We giggled again. "I know that's right," chimed Kiarra.

I tried to sneak away, but when dad said, "Hey Kosby come over here," I was stuck. I had to walk over there. With each step, my legs felt like tree trunks.

Kiara laughed, "Kosby, you're a fool!"

We both laughed at that statement. I continued with my story. "So, I went over there." "This is my princess, Kosby," Dad said. "Dad introduced me to his friends; some I knew, others I didn't. I said, *"hello, gentlemen,"* so I wouldn't have to speak to each man individually. I looked at Deion. He had his poker face on; I didn't know what to do. It was crazy because, until that moment, I hadn't even known his first name.

We had a good time together; it was just like I'd known this man my entire life. After we sat and talked, I thought maybe he might be fun to hang around. I guess he thought the same thing because he stayed with me all evening. I think we both felt very comfortable. Kiarra, that party was a success. I worked hard at planning dad's party. Don't know if I want to do that again, at least not real soon. But I must admit it was a lot of fun for everybody, and girl DJ Phire was off the hook."

I had a similar conversation with Stacy. My girl and I laughed, but she was the one that announced the exciting news. She told me she was pregnant, and she and Carl were very excited.

"Congratulations, oh my gosh. I'm going to be an aunt."

Stacy giggled. "Girl, I know you're going to be all over this baby. That's why we decided to ask you to be the godmother."

"Shut the front door. Yes, I'd be happy to be the godmother."

"It was hard at the party watching everybody drink and not explain that I was the designated driver because all I had was 7up and cranberry juice in a cocktail glass."

This girl had me giggling. I had so much fun talking with her. Stacey wanted me to come over and help her design the baby's room.

"You know you got that panache. Everyone doesn't have it when it comes to decorating."

"Thank you, Stacey. That made my day. It's been wonderful talking to you, my friend."

We set a date for me to go over and help with the baby's room. Then we'd go shopping for a neutral color because it was too early to know if it would be a boy or girl.

"Cool, we got this, and with you being an obstetrician, you can deliver your own baby," I joked.

"You know what? I told Carl you would say that. Believe me, girl, I know your personality. You are too funny."

I couldn't believe how well things were going for all of us. It rarely happened when we had a moment where someone didn't have a crisis. I hoped my entire world didn't come tumbling down at one time. I don't know if I could handle that. In the meantime, I would look for baby furniture, and, of course, I'd have to plan a baby shower.

Chapter Six

Derrick

I'd been going out with Kiarra a couple of months now, and things were getting better between us. I was attracted to her looks in the beginning, but she was so much more than good looks. She was fun, vivacious, smart, caring, and she could cook.

As a police officer, she was always concerned about my safety. I told her to quit worrying because I just passed the detective exam and was hoping to get promoted soon. Not that detectives don't get hurt in the line of duty, but they're less likely to get shot at like an officer. We celebrated the night I told her. We spent most of our free time together.

Just last weekend, we went to her girlfriend Kosby's retirement party for her dad. The party was at Caesars Palace, and they pulled out all the bells and whistles. It was an after-five affair. Kiarra was the ultimate lady. I believe she only had one real drink and a glass of champagne when Kosby's father cut his cake.

Her other girlfriend, Stacey, sat at the table with us. Both she and her husband Carl were doctors. Unbelievable. I could only imagine what kind of money they made. I enjoyed being with her friends. It sure beat the ghetto where I grew up. I remember worrying about having something to eat; we never had new clothes. I promised myself back then I would do good in school and get a decent-paying job. When I had my family, I would be there to take care of them. That's what I see in Kiarra. She's a wonderful woman. It would be in the world I always wanted to live. She would be a great mother.

Tonight, we were going bowling; I hoped she liked it. I know it's not fancy like what her friends do, but the police officers have a team, and we're pretty good. I've been a member of the team for three years now. Two of the years, we won the national title. Most of the officers bring their girlfriends, and they have a little group of officer wives and girlfriends that do all kinds of things together. I hoped she cliqued with them; she might be too sophisticated considering the friends she hung around. In my mind, those things were trivial. It was the relationship she and I had that was important. I think I finally had my Love Jones.

I got dressed and was off to pick up my girl. Around my friends, I always felt like I was at the top of the mountain, but her friends were so bougie, I felt like the scum of the year. I hoped she didn't end up in a fancy dress when I picked her up, or I'd have to tell her when you bowl, you wear jeans. I should have mentioned that to her when we talked on the phone, but I didn't think about it. She was probably used to getting dressed up for everything.

I parked my car, walked up to her apartment, and rang the doorbell. She opened the door. I was surprised she was wearing a t-shirt, jeans, and tennis shoes. I was happy I had this lady. She wasn't bougie. She understood how regular people lived. That's another thing I love about her. Wow, I just thought about the L-word. She could be the one for me.

"You look nice," I told her.

"Thank you, so do you," she said.

"Are you ready to go?"

"Yes, I am. Let me grab my jacket."

Kiarra shut and locked her door. I held her hand as we walked to the car. I opened her door. She got in. I jogged over to the driver's side, and we were on our way. We got there in no time. I introduced her to my friends. She handled herself as she spoke to them and had conversations with their ladies. She drank a beer just like everyone else, and to my disbelief, she could actually bowl.

"You've done this before, haven't you?" I asked.

Kiarra gave me a dazzling smile. "Yes, I used to be in a bowling league when I was in middle school, my friends, and I loved bowling. As a matter of fact, I think we tried all kinds of sports we played lacrosse, tennis, soccer, gymnastics, and golf. Can you play that many sports?"

"No, I can't. I played t-ball as a kid, and then baseball. When I got to high school, I loved basketball, but there were a lot of sports I couldn't play. One thing I regret is I don't know how to swim."

"You don't know how to swim, that's unbelievable. I must teach you."

"No, you can't teach an old dog new tricks."

We both laughed. She must have been my good luck charm because I had one of my highest scores ever. Naturally, my team won.

"That was so much fun," she said.

"Yes, it was. I enjoyed every minute. I bet you this year we retake the trophy again," I said.

"That would be nice, three years in a row, right?"

"Yes, but the next team we're playing, they are some talented bowlers."

"You know you got this. Your team can beat them with one hand tied behind your backs."

"No, they really are a force to be reckoned with; they were National Champions for five years until we won two years ago. We beat them by a mere two points."

"Are you hungry," she asked.

"Yes, something to eat would be nice."

"Okay, make yourself a drink, I'll go into the kitchen and get dinner started."

I walked over to the bar. I pulled out a beer from the mini-fridge. I had been drinking beer at the bowling alley, and being a police officer, the last thing I needed was a DUI. I didn't know what she was cooking, but it sure smelled good. Kiarra came out of the kitchen, platters in hand. She had made a salad, broiled some pork chops, rice, she even had some soft French bread. We sat down at her table and held hands while she prayed. Afterward, we began to eat the wonderful meal she cooked. Kiarra looked at me and smiled.

"You know I enjoy cooking for you. When I'm by myself, I might sit down and have a bowl of cereal, but when I was growing up, I would cook for my whole family. I was the oldest, plus, with my mom being a single parent, I had to step up. I always made sure to make her a plate. I would put it in the oven so she could eat when she got home. You know, my mom was hardworking, not an easy day at our house because she worked two jobs and would get up early in the morning, then she wouldn't get home until late in the evening. The good part was, she had weekends off. We still had a lot of fun together on the weekends. Plus, I wasn't stuck taking care of all the kids. I can remember my father when I was very young, but who knows what happened to him. I never bugged my mom about it because she always looked stressed if I brought it up. I guess that's why I don't have any children now because I needed that time to be alone. Funny, now that I'm comfortable, happy, and have a good man. I could see myself one day being a mom." she said.

"Yeah, it's a lot easier for men. After all, women carry the child for nine months and go through childbirth. I can't even imagine. Many moms not only take care of their children, but they work. In this economy, it's hard to live off one income, even a decent income. But children seem to keep raising themselves, and people still seem to keep having more. You should see what I see on the streets. The kids join gangs to belong. The gangs become their family. Either there was no family at home because they were working, or they have some mother who sits on her butt all day. I can at least respect a mother who's forced to work too much and can't raise her children.

I don't know how to put this, but I can't honestly say that slavery went anywhere, it's just a whole new group of people in it. There's hardly any middle class anymore. They took the high paying hardworking, no education jobs out of America, and sent them over to Mexico and Asia and anywhere they could get cheap labor.

But they're paying for it because we must buy back everything that America used to make. Now the Chinese are buying up all of America, and our economy is so far into debt I doubt if we'd ever catch up. History has shown us the only way to get rid of that debt is war, and that scares me to no end." I said.

"I know what you mean, the top three percent of the world rule every country. They decide when there will be a recession, and they control the banks. The best way to make it in this country is to stay out of debt. I say don't use your credit card, pay for your stuff with cash, and save up for your car. Everybody doesn't need a new car. My friend Kosby, for example has a 2018 Cadillac. It's the small one, the most affordable one, but nevertheless, that's too darn much money for a car. I say buy a car that's already depreciated and pay cash, then you don't have a car note. I know I'm saving up my money; one day I want to have a house. I don't want a beautiful condo like what Kosby has, and I don't need a mansion like Stacey and Carl have; I want a regular people house and that should be my only bill." she said.

"We do think alike," I said. "The best thing a person could do is to stay out of debt because staying out of debt keeps you out of slavery. They show you commercials on TV 24/7, make you think you must have the best everything; the newest iPhone, red bottom high heels, certain makeup, Gucci shoes. We don't need that stuff. A basic pair of pants and a shirt is all anyone needs. That's another reason I appreciate being a patrol officer because I wear a uniform and I don't have to trip about my wardrobe. I will have to buy suits when I become a detective, but that'll be an investment." We talked the night away, hitting it off.

Chapter Seven

Deion

I was so excited about getting ready for my date with Kosby. I took a nice long shower, put on my favorite cologne, combed my hair, and put a little gel in it to make the waves pop. I called Kosby on the phone to see if she was about ready, and she said yes. So, I grabbed my leather jacket and caught the elevator down two floors.

She looked breathtaking wearing a gold and black mesh top, nice fitting black straight leg jeans, and some sexy bootie sandals. She grabbed a gold jacket, and we were out the door. I took her to Morton's Steakhouse. Dinner was on point; I was so intrigued by our conversation. We felt like old friends. I could talk to Kosby about anything. The mere melodic sound of her speech sent chills through my body. Now for my big surprise, I was taking her to T-Mobile to see Jay-Z. I was glad we had a hearty meal because we waited in line for two hours before they let us in to be seated. I'd gone all out for this date.

Vic Mensa opened the show; he was alright. I only knew his one hit. After Vic Mensa finished, Jay-Z appeared. I could see the anticipation in the crowd as that song 'Beach was Better' vibrated through my feet up to my body, and everyone cheered in unison. I watched Kosby swing her hips from side to side as vendors tried to sell beer in the aisle. The song faded to 'Niggas in Paris' featuring Kanye West. Everyone began rapping along with Jay-Z. The mood was off the hook. The show only got better because my favorite song, 'On to The Next One' started. He gave a tribute to Chester from Linkin Park and talked about suicide. Jay-Z's part of the show was two hours, and when he finished, he said,

"I'll see ya'll later. I'm going to the crap table."

Kosby and I were pumped as we followed the crowd out of the arena. We headed to the parking lot to get my car.

"Do you still feel like partying?" I asked.

"Sure, what do you have in mind," she asked.

"Let's go dancing," I replied.

So, we traveled down the street to Town Square, parked, and walked to the Blue Martini. The club was popping, and people were dancing. Their live band played, and the lead singer was *sanging* them songs. I led Kosby to the dance floor.

"Do you know how to do Chicago-style stepping?

"Yeah, let's do it."

By the time the song ended, we heard clapping from the crowd that had gathered around us. We went back to our seats, enjoyed our drinks as we laughed, talked, and laughed some more.

"I couldn't have asked for a better date," I told her. She was so breathtaking. Brothers turned around to look at her everywhere we went. Kosby is the one, I thought. It was getting late. We decided it was time to go home. Good thing we lived only a short drive away.

Chapter Eight

Kosby

I had a wonderful time on my date with Deion. I couldn't believe how he went all out for me; I was tickled pink. That's the way a man is supposed to treat a lady!

Deion had to be my soulmate. He'd included everything that anyone could want on their first date. He was so sweet. I told him I would take him out for the next date. I had to think of something good. Maybe I could find a good movie. I needed to think of something good to entertain him.

The evening was beautiful. When he walked me to my door, I couldn't wait for our first kiss. I closed my eyes, and I never wanted to stop. I don't think he did either. I finally said goodnight. I thanked him for such a good time. And I meant every word.

After I crawled out of bed in the afternoon, I seriously needed to get some exercise in. So, I went down to the gym to run on the treadmill. Deion was in there working out; I guess that's the downside to us living in the same building. I giggled every time I thought about how he tried to show off. He was working every muscle on his toned body, and he looked good. If he only knew he didn't have to do all that for me because I already enjoyed looking at every inch of him. I did a half an hour on the treadmill, he was still working out when I finished, but he interrupted his workout to come over and speak to me.

"Hey babe, how you are today?" he asked.

"I'm good now that I see you." His grin covered his face. I could see all his perfect teeth.

"What are you doing later?"

"Nothing. We had a big night last night, so I planned to rest this evening. But you're more than welcome to come down to watch a movie with me if you'd like.

"Sure, that would be fun."

"Okay, I'll pop us some popcorn," I said.

I went home, cleaned my house from top to bottom, and then hopped in the shower. When I got out, I checked to make sure I had a selection of beverages. Whenever he got here, I would be ready.

It wasn't long before he showed up looking good in a pair of khaki slacks, t-shirt and he was rocking a new pair of Nikes. I invited him into the living area as he looked around.

"Your place is gorgeous. Who did you use as an interior decorator?"

"I didn't use an interior decorator. I did this all by my little old self."

"You got skills, girl. I know you may be a great actuary, but I bet you'd make just as much money in interior design because you got it going on."

I laughed because it was alright; let me stop lying. I knew my place looked good. I'd been waiting for my girlfriends to come over and see my home, but I hadn't seen either of them in a while.

"I need you to come over and decorate my place. This is awesome."

I smiled again. "Oh, come on now, it's alright, but it isn't all that."

"Kosby, this condo could be featured on one of those old episodes of Cribs."

We both broke out laughing. We were in a giggly mood. I handed him the remote.

"Here, pick out a movie."

We couldn't stop laughing. We were silly. We curled up together.

"Are you hungry," I questioned, knowing good and well he was because we hadn't eaten any dinner.

I pull out three salmon fillets and put them on the Foreman grill. I fixed corn on the cob and made a nice salad to complete the meal. We were sitting at the table in less than 30 minutes.

"This is delicious and so juicy. I love salmon," he offered.

"Thank you. I'm glad you like salmon. I marinated them earlier using my mom's recipe."

"I bet your mom can throw down."

"Yes, she can cook. I always wanted to cook like her. So, I would help her every chance she gave me. When I went to school and moved off campus, my friends would buy food and bring it over, and we would have dinners like that movie, Soul Food. Where did you go to school, Deion?"

"I graduated from the United States Air Force Academy; it's a little north of Colorado Springs. I was commissioned as a second lieutenant when I received my Bachelor of Science degree. It was awesome starting my career off as an officer. I ate my meals in the mess hall. They tasted so good too because we never had enough food at home. I had a commitment to the Air Force for education. I felt like I'd do 20 years before I retired, but the airline kept pursuing me, the money they offered was good, and I took it. After finishing my commitment with the Air Force, I signed up with the United States Air Force National Guard."

"Wow, I know your mother was proud of you."

"Yes, she was because the school in the hood was so easy. I always had a 4.0-grade point average, and it paid off when I applied for the Air Force Academy. Except I didn't realize how behind I was from school until everything was so hard. They were all AP classes. I didn't even know what an AP class was. Thank goodness there was a Black professor who took a liking to me and helped me understand all the lessons. I learned fast, and to everyone's amazement, I ended up in the top five percent of my class.

"That's amazing. You overcame all the odds, and now you're a success. I know you're busy, but you should mentor a young man to give back to the community the same way your professor mentored you." I said.

"That's easier said than done. I offered my time to tutor the Clark County school system. I was insulted when the lady wanted to know if I had any sex offender charges. Then they told me they couldn't use my help because of my unpredictable schedule. So, you don't have to wonder why they have the lowest rated public-school system in America."

I was at a loss for words. "The Bible said, 'Woe to those who call evil good and good evil, who put darkness for light and light for his darkness.' This world is so mixed up, but you shouldn't take it personally. They are trying to protect the children against pedophiles. They should have asked you if you could commit to a certain day at a particular time before they even gave you the paperwork. That would have ended the whole thing, no mountain of paperwork, background checks, or national pedophile checks."

Deion smiled at me. "You are an optimist. You find the good in everything. You're right; it's all about the delivery. She treated me negatively, and that was probably how she lived her whole life." he said.

"Miserable, and she wanted you to be miserable, too. Not everyone who volunteered to help had an ulterior motive of being a pervert or a pedophile." I added.

Deion stood up, "I better get going now; I have an early flight in the morning."

I grabbed his hand and walked him to the door.

"Thank you for dinner. It was delicious. The movie was thrilling; your company was magnificent." he said.

"I enjoyed our evening together, too."

Deion went in for a kiss. I joined in. We said our goodbyes. I fell upon the back of the locked door to catch my breath from the steamy kiss.

Chapter Nine

Kiarra

I had been so busy at work that I hadn't had time to see Derrick. Honestly, I'd been avoiding Derrick. I enjoyed spending time with him, but I was noticing that a little of him goes a long way. I didn't know if it was because he was a police officer, a man, or just a pure chauvinist. He thought the perfect woman cooked all the meals. It would be nice if he would take me out to dinner sometime or go to a movie or a play. He refused to spend a little money on me. He was single and lived in a bachelor's apartment. Still, he's always acted like he was so broke. I didn't know if he was frugal from having such a hard childhood, but my childhood wasn't exactly great, either. He came over here like he was paying the bills, yet has not offered me any grocery money. And still expected me to cook for him every time he showed up.

I'm sure that's why I am still single. I find something wrong with every man I date. Well, at least he isn't as bad as Drew was. Drew claimed he got laid off his job, but I don't think he ever worked more than a week in his life. Every time I saw him, he was begging me for money. I had to let him go. It was so bad I moved and changed my phone number. Good thing he couldn't get up to the office where I work; you need to have a special card to get in. I wondered what was wrong with me because I always attracted the wrong men. Derrick fooled me by buying me flowers and taking me out to eat on the first date, but believe me; he's never done it again.

Kosby never accepted any of the men I dated. I was sure she would always be alone or end up dating men of other nationalities because girlfriend never took any stuff. Kosby grew up as her daddy's princess, and mama spoiled her with anything she wanted. One thing I knew for sure, Kosby was a perfectionist. She was smart. She would look at Stacey and me and wonder why on earth we couldn't understand the assignment, or why we couldn't do the math. She would show us how to do the work then she would give us problem after problem until we could do it. Schoolwork, along with everything else, seemed to be easy for her. So, what was it about men she knew that I didn't know?

I was so happy when I met Derrick, a black man working. But he was such a chauvinist. He thought everything was man's work or woman's work. He talked about his fellow police officers who, were women. He'd say they ought to be at home, or they need to get a job in the office. I'm telling you that man lived in the Stone Age. After watching my mom work two jobs, I don't want a man that didn't have the right perspective of what a woman should be. I would talk to him and give it a chance. But if he didn't change, I'd be back to single Kiarra. I hadn't even told my friends how I felt because I wasn't sure they would understand. Stacey married an orthopedic surgeon, and Kosby was dating a pilot. Those were the kind of problems I'd like to have.

Chapter Ten

Kosby

I was so excited. This evening I would take Deion out. He was a perfect gentleman the night he came over to watch movies. Then one night, he invited me to his place while he grilled steaks on his patio. It was scrumptious.

His condo was beautiful. The walls were adorned with African American paintings. I was astonished to see how lovely his place was. I didn't expect him to have this kind of taste.

Tonight, much to my amazement, he bought me beautiful white orchids in a stunning vase. They were gorgeous.

"Thank you, Deion." I sat them on my dining room table.

"I love orchids; thank you so much." I kissed him on the cheek.

"You're welcome." His smile was wide.

We made it down to the garage and got in my car. I drove to Caesars Palace. We walked into the Old Homestead Steakhouse for dinner, upscale but comfortable. Deion and I enjoyed the scenery while sipping on cocktails. As we finished up our food, the Chef came out with two cheesecakes.

"Hi, Kosby, it's a joy to see you again. These cheesecakes are also on me."

"Thank you so much. Dinner was delicious; everything was prepared to perfection." I introduced him to my date.

We left Caesars Palace and went to the show. Ka was a beautiful story where the people spoke a made-up language. It was funny how even though you didn't understand one word, the motions were universal.

"What would you like to do now?" I questioned.

"I don't know. It was your turn to plan the date?"

I laughed. "Hey, let's go over to the slot machines." I put twenty dollars in his machine and twenty dollars in mine. We sat next to each other and played. At one point, he had lost his twenty I was up by forty, so I put another twenty-dollar bill in his machine. I knew this was my night because everything had gone perfect. I ended up hitting two hundred dollars that I cashed in, not giving them a chance to get it back. Afterward, he walked me to my front door.

"Thank you for such a lovely evening; you went all out. I appreciate it."

We smiled at each other and then he kissed me delicately.

Chapter Eleven

Deion

That woman is incredible. She took me on a great date. I don't remember any woman ever treating me like this. Kosby wouldn't let me pay for anything; her generosity was rewarded with winning two-hundred dollars in cash. Ka was beautiful; women seemed to love stuff like that. She ooh'd and aah'd all evening. The acrobatic talent amazed me, though. They had perfect bodies; it was phenomenal.

I had a two o'clock appointment with my pastor, so I made myself a sandwich and drank some lemonade. I had enough time to get there factoring in Vegas traffic. I parked and made my way into the church.

"Hello, Brother Deion, you can go right in, the pastor is waiting for you."

"Thank you," I said to the church secretary Nona, who's been here for over ten years.

"Good afternoon, Reverend Woods."

"Yes, it's a wonderful day Brother Deion, the Lord woke us up, didn't he?"

"Yes, he did pastor, and I'm thankful. I need to speak with you about a relationship I'm in with a wonderful lady."

"Okay, then, son. Tell me what's going on."

"I just met her a couple of months ago. She's the first woman that I think I could pursue in a long-term relationship. You know we don't have a physical relationship because of my belief in God. But I've been nervous about this because I don't want to lose her."

"Has she been pressuring you to have sex, son?" he asked.

"No, she hasn't, but I need some help on how to handle this. I think I've already waited too long because if she doesn't agree, I'll be heartbroken."

"Brother Deion, if she feels the same way about you, she'll wait."

"I know you're right. Things have been going well between us. I rarely date women this long because they get so upset about not having sex. One woman called me gay; she said it couldn't be her. It had to be something wrong with me."

Pastor chuckled, "What did you say to her?"

"I said if I were gay, I wouldn't be out with her; I'd be dating any man I wanted!"

We both fell out laughing. "Brother Deion, that was a great answer. Some women don't know a good man when they meet him because they are not good women."

"Thank you, pastor, I feel better already."

"I believe you have a good woman, if she were after sex, she would have already been gone, or she would have at least tried to get you in bed. Talk to her. I bet you'll discover she is a woman of God." He shook my hand, and I left the church, feeling more confident.

I called Kosby and invited her over to my house. She agreed to come right up. I nervously paced the floor about this conversation. Either I would be on cloud nine when she left, or I would be single and not so ready to mingle. I heard the doorbell ringing.

"Hi, sweetie." I kissed her on the cheek.

"Hi, babe, how are you? What's so crucial that you needed to talk to me?" She questioned.

"Well, it's something I should have talked to you about when we first met. I am a Christian, and I tell you I would never have been where I am today had it not been for our Heavenly Father. I dedicated my life to God. I read my Bible daily, and I pray. I try to treat others the same way I would treat myself. That is the commandment that Jesus asked of us. At my church, we don't believe in having premarital sex. I didn't want you to think something was wrong with me because after we finish our dates, I kiss you and go home. Believe me, I'm looking at you baby, and really, I have a hard time leaving. But if this is something you can't handle, I thought it would be best that I talk to you about it now."

"Oh Deion, yeah we should have talked about this earlier, you would have realized I don't have a problem with it. Ever wonder why I never invited you in at the end of an evening to have a nightcap, or why I always kissed you at the door before I opened it? We were both doing the same thing. I was brought up in the church, and I have never strayed — everything I have I give the glory to God. I thought you might have understood the other night when I quoted you scripture from the Bible. No baby, we are good. I am happy because we're on the same accord. Now, tell me what church you go to, and I'll tell you all about mine."

"I tell you what, Kosby, we can do better than that. You know because of my job I can't go to church every Sunday so my next free Sunday I'll go to church with you and then the following Sunday I have off you can go to church with me. Together we can talk about the churches and decide which one we would like to attend together. See, I know we've only been seeing each other a couple of months now, but from the very first moment when that elevator broke, and you snapped the selfie of us, I knew you were the woman for me. I'd been looking for you my whole adult life. As we spent time together, talked, and did things together, I knew you were my soulmate. Most women want to date a pilot because of the money, but I bet you anything you probably make more money than I do. You were kind enough to take me out without giving it a second thought, and that's what I'm looking for in a woman. Someone I can share with, you know, fifty, fifty? I would never expect you to cook my dinner every night. Well, I'm not home every night, but when I'm home, I'd love to cook for you sometimes, and sometimes you cook for me. If we don't feel like cooking, we'll go somewhere and eat. I met your parents, and, on Sunday, you visit my church. I want to take you over to meet my mom. She'll be excited to meet you because I never brought a woman home before."

"Wow, you have made me so happy!" she squealed. "I never thought I'd find a man who could live up to what I expected from a mate. But you have. I feel committed to you, and I hope you feel the same way about me. Don't be afraid to talk to me about anything. Let's always be truthful with each other because not being truthful destroys good relationships."

"Yes, Kosby, you're right."

Chapter Twelve

Derrick

So, I called Kiarra. She hasn't called me back. I think something's wrong because this has been going on for a few days now. I was sure she was avoiding me, yet I couldn't figure out what I did. After all, I was the model man. Any woman in their right mind would be lucky to have me. I was one of Las Vegas' best. I was a Las Vegas Police Officer, so what was wrong with her? That's exactly why she's been sitting up there with no man. She obviously didn't know how to keep one.

She could cook and clean, she worked a good job, so what's her problem? I called earlier, and she didn't answer. Her phone went straight to voicemail. I went by her apartment; she didn't even answer the door. I knocked on some of her neighbor's doors to see if anyone had seen her, and everyone told me yes, she goes to work every day. I asked had anyone seen her leave today, but they all said no. So, I know she's in there. She's hiding from me. Well, I'm not the one to be treated like that! All these chicks around here that want to get with me? I'd scratch her name off my list, and she'd never hear from me again. I can't stand stupid ass, Black women.

I got to work, but my partner called in sick. They put a rookie with me. Man, could this day get any worse? I knew I should have been more patient, but rookies get on my nerves. They were always asking how you do this and how did you do that. How did you make it through Police Academy if you didn't know how to do a darn thing? But I don't complain. I treat them nice; I show them how to get the job done. I don't think most of them ever made it six months. Dumbasses. I decided to give this girl another call since she really was the best thing that happened to me in a long time. Most of the women I got with had five or more kids. Every one of them had a different daddy. Their houses were dirty. They didn't have any jobs. But I tell you what, their hair and nails were done; they had great clothes, yet their kids were running around in a diaper. So, here I find a great woman, no kids, and she doesn't appreciate me? Well, I hope she dies an old maid.

The rookie had been working hard today. I had him driving while I sat back, giving him directions to follow. We got a call not far from our current location. We arrived at the scene, and some old homeless woman was shoplifting in 7-Eleven. I don't get that. If you're going to go to jail for shoplifting, why wouldn't you go to a store like Macy's or Nordstrom? No, we get people that go to 7-Eleven and steal bags of

Cheetos. I asked the manager what she took, and he handed me a bag of Cheetos.

"Let the woman go," I said.

The manager said, "no, I want you to take her to jail because she'll just be back tomorrow."

I looked at the woman. "Now, if I pay for your bag of Cheetos, will you promise not to come back to this store?"

"Yes, sir, no, I won't come back," she said.

"Call me personally if this lady comes back to your store." I gave my card to the manager.

We left, and I told the rookie, "It's not worth all the paperwork we'd have to fill out over a bag of Cheetos. She was probably trying to go to jail anyway. If she's hungry, she knows she'd get three meals and a cot in jail. I'm sure after sleeping on the streets. Jail beats her hell any day of the week.

These homeless people will try anything to go to jail. Some of them have rap sheets as long as your whole body. They don't care. Most of them need to be put away in mental institutions. But they did away with all the institutions, letting the crazies walk the street. They don't comb their hair; they'll lay right there in the street. I tell you they're not dealing with a full deck of cards. I got back in the car with my partner.

"We'd be lucky if that was the most exciting thing that happened to us today." Just as I said that a car rolled down the street, going

60 miles an hour in 35 miles an hour zone. I called it in while the rookie turned on the siren and then pulled the man over.

"Ask him for his license and registration I got you covered from the back; you watch him every moment. Make sure he's not reaching for anything like a gun. Got that rookie?"

He said, "Yes, got it. I was sure he could handle that."

He walked up to the car, and as soon as he got to the window, the driver took off, he ran back to the car, and the chase was on.

"Yes, this is car 143. We have a '10-80', chase in progress. The suspect is speeding down Flamingo. We are requesting a '10-78' officer needs assistance." The car was going about 90 miles an hour up the Boulder Highway. Then the vehicle crashed into a semi-truck and flipped over.

"Pull out your gun and go investigate, I'll call for an ambulance." After notifying all the proper authorities, I ran to the car to assist my partner. He was doing just fine; the perpetrator would have to be cut out of this car when the fire department arrived. I looked at the accident, *you big dummy*, I thought. If you don't die of your injuries, you'll probably be a vegetable. Once the fire department arrived, they put cones around the entire area to stop traffic. My partner and I directed traffic around the scene the old-fashioned way, with hand signals. It was hot. I couldn't wait for this day to end.

Chapter Thirteen

Kosby

Things were going well between Deion and me. Ever since we had that talk and found out, we were on the same page with our relationship. Things have flourished. We've been spending a lot of time together. This evening while Deion was working, I was going out with the girls. It had been such a long time since we all got together. With Stacey being pregnant, our girls' nights would start comprising of just Kiarra and me. Tonight, we were going to the South Point Hotel and Casino for Gregg Austin's Motown Review. I enjoyed going there because we were all raised on oldies. Our parents played those records, and I tell you to this day we could sing every word. My favorite was Smokey Robinson, Kiarra loved Marvin Gaye, and Stacey was crazy about Diana Ross.

It was a lovely scene. They had a dance floor right in front of the stage. Almost everyone that went were regulars. The floor featured line dances and every spinoff of the Electric Slide you could imagine. We got silly and went out on the Dance Floor to join in on the fun.

I don't know how I went so long without

seeing my girls because we used to do this all the time. We had a different spot to hit every night of the week. We were a lot older now. After the band finished singing, the DJ put on music while the band took a break. Everybody and their momma were on the floor doing the Wobble. We were laughing, and giggling, Kiarra joined us on the dance floor.

The floor was packed, Wobble baby, Wobble baby. We had such an enjoyable time, but, like all good things, the evening ended.

The next morning, my shower was so refreshing, and the hot water hit the spot. Plus, my headache was gone. Thank you, Advil. I wasted no time putting on my professional attire.

At my desk, my phone rang. It was Deion.

"How are you doing? I miss you. I just wanted to tell you to hang in there. I'll be home tomorrow."

"I'm doing fine. I miss you too!" We chatted a little while longer, I hung up and got back to work.

After work, I went shopping. I needed a cute outfit for church Sunday since Deion was going with me. My mother told me to bring him over for Sunday dinner. I was excited about that. I found a beautiful satin dress with a matching jacket; a soft green I knew Deion would love this dress.

It was Sunday morning. It thrilled me to

bring Deion to my church. I got up early so I wouldn't have to rush. I had all my clothes laid out. I oiled up my body, put on my fragrance, and got dressed. I looked in my full-length mirror. I was pleased.

I got on the elevator, went up two floors, and rang Deion's doorbell. He answered. He looked scrumptious in his gray suit, and wouldn't you know it a light green shirt that made it look like we tried to dress alike. He had on a beautiful tie that picked up both the gray and green he was wearing.

"I can't believe we dressed like The Bobbsey Twins, Deion," I said.

He teased, "I know, what a coincidence. It shows we will have a great day together."

"I know that's right," I chirped. "Are you ready to go?"

"Yes, I'm ready. Let me lock up, and I'm all yours, madam."

We got in my car, and I drove us to church.

The pastor said on the microphone, "This is the day the Lord has made, let's rejoice and be glad in it."

Then the processional started; that's where everyone sings. The pastor walked up to the sanctuary, followed by the presiding elder, four reverends, and an evangelist. Then the choir followed, as everyone took their seats. The church service was beautiful. The choir did an excellent job. My favorite part of the service was the sermon the pastor gave. It was about a disabled man who laid in front of the temple daily. Every day he waited for someone going to the temple to provide him with charity.

The temple was named Beautiful, and the pastor said it was the ugliest beautiful temple. It took me a minute to understand what he was talking about, but he broke it down. I'd never forgotten how something so beautiful could be ugly. When people would go worship, the disabled man would lay there, and people would walk around him, or even step over him. They ignored him. Still, every single day someone picked him up, and every morning they brought him back where he laid on the ground in front of the temple. Then one day Peter and John went to the temple, and the disabled man asked for charity, they told him they didn't have any silver or gold, but they had something for him that was even better. They prayed for him in the name of Jesus, and the man was healed. Now this man had been disabled since birth, and we knew that he was over 40 years old, so he spent his whole life as a disabled person, they told him in the name of Jesus Christ to get up and walk. Peter took him by the right hand, lifted him up, and instantly his feet, and ankle bones were healed.

The man leaped up in the air, he walked, he entered the temple, and he jumped for joy. He praised God. The pastor said, remember, all blessings come from God.

After communion, it wasn't much longer before the service was over. The pastor stood at the door as we walked out, and I introduced him to Deion. The pastor shook his hand and said, "welcome, please come back."

We got in my car, and I drove him over to my parents' house.

"This is my parents' home. We eat Sunday dinner together. I am sure my brother Chris would be here with Sheila, his girlfriend."

Walking into the house, I said, "Hello," I heard voices saying hello back to me. "You all remember Deion, don't you?" I asked.

My father answered, "Of course I do. I worked with him for several years."

My mom came in and gave us hugs. My brother Chris stood up and hugged me and shook Deion's hand. Deion smiled at Chris's girlfriend.

"Something smells delicious," Deion said.

"Come on, Deion, have a seat; we're watching the game," my brother Chris offered.

I took my jacket off, got an apron out of the pantry, went to the sink, and washed my hands.

"What do you need me to do, mom?" I asked.

"Why don't you make the cornbread?"

"Okay," I said, grabbing the ingredients,

mixing them in a bowl. Stirring and listening to my mother and aunt talk.

"Mama, I finished the cornbread, but it still needs to go in the oven, is there anything else that you want me to prepare?"

"No, Kosby. We've got everything prepared. Now, we have to wait for what's baking to finish, put the new stuff in the oven, and then dinner will be ready. Why don't you go back to the living room and join the family?" she said.

I went back into the living room; there wasn't a seat anywhere. I sat on the ottoman right next to Deion. As they watched the game, I played on my phone. I texted Stacey. I was fascinated because everything was about this new baby that would join this world. I was going to be the godmother. So, this baby would be so spoiled. I was so anxious I almost felt like I was with child myself. I looked up at Deion and thought maybe one day I would? I played the game Words with Friends and hoped dinner would be ready soon.

"Kosby, can you set the table?" Mom asked.

I put down enough plates for everybody; I added the napkins, silverware, and then the glasses. I went into the kitchen, grabbed a pitcher of lemonade and a pitcher of iced tea.

After I finished the chores, she gave, me I told everyone to wash their hands for dinner.

My dad said, "Perfect timing, Kosby, the

game just went off."

All this food I just ate. I gotta workout really hard next week. I thought.

How's your food?" I asked Deion.

He smiled, "This food is delicious. It's been a long time since I've had a good soul food dinner. I need to workout hard at the gym this week." He patted his belly. "But I will enjoy myself today," he said.

"That's what I was thinking, but that's every week for me after Sunday dinner with mom."

"I didn't see them at church today. I guess they needed plenty of time to cook all this food."

"Our church has two services. The first one was at 8 a.m.; my parents always go to that one. The second service was the one you and I attended."

My mom asked, "How's everyone doing anybody want anything else?"

Deion replied, "Yes, I would love more of those oxtails."

I looked at him and laughed.

Chapter Fourteen

Kiarra

Why don't men get it? When you stop taking their calls, stop answering the door, don't accept their phone calls at work that you no longer want to be bothered. I thought I was so blessed to meet Derrick, but no. He may as well have been another bum.

He hooked me with one dinner at a five-star restaurant, and a bouquet of cheap grocery store flowers, but had never treated me again. He was no different from the other man I dated who wanted to live off me because he didn't want to work. He always had something smart to say about my girlfriends; he acted like our relationship wouldn't be like this if it wasn't for my bougie friends.

I wanted him to know that I was an around the way, girl. I grew up in the ghetto. I came from a family with no money. But I worked hard to get out of that, and even though I bypassed college, I had a good job. I worked every day. I made it to the top of my field. I felt very fortunate to be where I was today, so I'd be darn if I let some man walk into my life and think they would spend all my money and act like a Scrooge when it came to treating me. I just had enough of Derrick. I couldn't understand why he wouldn't take the hint. What else could I do to show him I didn't want to be bothered?

No, I hadn't met another man, at least not yet. And if it was God's will, I might not ever meet that man. But I was okay with that as long as I had peace in my world. I haven't talked to my girls about this problem, but today I was going to confide in my friend Kosby. I knew Kosby was the right friend to talk to because she went forever without a man, and she was happy. If he couldn't treat her the way she wanted to be treated, she treated herself. She told me that all the time and I knew she was right.

I used to think she would never find a man because her expectations were too high. I believed if she found a man, he wouldn't be Black, but she held on to her expectations, and now she had a great boyfriend. He seemed to love her the same way she loved him. They had so much fun together. He took her out, bought her flowers, and in return, she did the same for him. They were to the point where they were going to each other's churches.

I grew up in the church, but somewhere along the line, I stopped going. Now that I look back at it, that could be why I could never find the perfect man for me. Well, I was so through with Derrick, I changed my cell phone number, and I hoped he found someone that would make him happy. I just wasn't the one.

I looked out the window to make sure I didn't see any police cars outside. The coast seemed clear, so I grabbed my purse and my keys, locked my apartment and jumped into my car because I was meeting Kosby for lunch. No sooner than I turned the corner, a siren went off. I looked in my rearview mirror to see the blue lights flashing at me, so I pulled over. I knew it was that fool, Derrick because I hadn't broken any traffic laws. Sure, enough, here he comes walking to my car.

"What's up, Kiarra," he inquired.

"Nothing, Derrick. Is there a reason you stopped me?"

"Yes, I want to know why you changed your phone number and why you're avoiding me?"

"It just wasn't working out between us, Derrick. I'd rather just be alone."

"Don't lie, Kiarra. I treated you like a Queen. I bet your bougie friends set you up with one of their bougie friends. Right!"

"Derrick, it's that kind of warped thinking that made me stop feeling you. The only place you ever took me was bowling. Otherwise, you were at my apartment, eating up all my food. You never even offered to help me with groceries. Your cheap, selfish, and chauvinistic; attributes I'm not particularly looking for in a man. And for the record, I am not seeing anyone else. I want you to understand I don't want to see you either. So, go back to your car and do the job you are getting paid to do or write me a ticket so that I can file a complaint against you with the police department."

I could see the hurt on his face before he turned around and walked back to his car. I put my car in drive. I was back on the task of meeting Kosby for lunch. We gave the waitress our orders. I told Kosby about the problems I was having with Derrick.

"When I met him, I was so happy. I was mesmerized. I didn't recognize any of his character flaws. But they were more than I could handle, we did the same things all the time.

I got so tired of cooking for him. He never bought me flowers. He never did anything special for me. Kosby, the thing that irritated me the most was he called you and Stacey my bougie friends. I got so irritated I could hardly stand to sit there with him. Even the stories he told me about his job were chauvinistic, and he couldn't see it.

I don't know how he ever made it through the police academy. He doesn't think women should have any jobs or responsibilities other than sitting at a desk working for a man. See, he threw my job at me all the time. He would say, 'Administrative assistant, you're just a secretary, girl.' Feeling the way I did, I knew I would have to break up with Derrick. That's the real reason I changed my phone number, but he's been coming by my house knocking on my door, I couldn't play any music, I couldn't turn on my TV. I just went into my bedroom to relax because I didn't want to be bothered.

And the coup de gras was he had the audacity to ask my neighbors if they had seen me and if I still lived there. Now I couldn't let him go without a confrontation because he stalked me. The reason I was late meeting you this afternoon was because when I got in my car and turned the corner, he hit me with the blue lights and pulled me over. I knew it would be him, so girl, I had to threaten him."

Our food came, and we both ate in silence for a moment.

"Awe Kiarra, I had no idea you were going through this with that man. Why did you take so long to confide in me? I thought we were like sisters."

"I know, sweetie. At first, I was content. Looking back, there were plenty of red flags. I ignored them. But as time went on, I realized I was miserable with him. It got to the point I couldn't stand to hear him talk. I'm not a fighter Kosby you know that, so I would bite my tongue. I woke up one day and realized this was something I could no longer do; I was much happier alone."

"I agree with you. Derrick sounds like he needs professional help. There's nothing you or I could do to help him. I'm glad you got away from him because he sounds so resentful. He may try to retaliate."

"Yes, that was my fear, too. I hate going home."

"Why don't I go with you to your apartment? You can pack a bag and come stay with me for a while until he cools down."

"Thank you, Kosby, but I don't want to mess up your groove with Deion."

"You won't be messing up our groove, sweetheart. Deion is a pilot like dad, and he's gone a lot. When he is at home, he stays at his place, and I stay at mine."

"Don't tell me you haven't given him some; I always thought that was the reason you couldn't keep a man."

Kosby laughed, "You're probably right, but that was always okay with me. He didn't love me anyway if he couldn't wait. But Deion and I are on the same accord; we have the same values. You should come back to church, pray, and tell our Heavenly Father the kind of man you want, be specific, and then walk in faith. By that, I mean, you only need to ask God one time, because He will bless you, but it will be on His time. Believe."

"You know that's why I love you like a sister; you always tell it like it is. You don't sugar coat it; in other words, a duck is a duck." Kosby looked at me crazy, and we fell out laughing. It felt good. I hadn't laughed in a long time.

Chapter Fifteen

Deion

My life has changed since meeting Kosby. I looked forward to coming home and seeing her. Before meeting her, my thrill was flying the plane and seeing so many places. I spent a lot of time traveling on my days off. But since I met Kosby, I couldn't wait to get back to Vegas. I wasn't a gambling man, so other than my job, mother, and church, nothing more much interested me. I enjoyed visiting my mother; I bought her a small ranch home with three bedrooms and two bathrooms, which was excellent for her. I came from a big family, and one of my brothers or sisters was always visiting her, and she loved them visiting.

When I got home, I called my girlfriend.

"Hey, I'm back," I said as I stretched out on the couch.

"I'm happy to hear your voice. It seemed like you'd be away forever."

"Why don't I come down so we can get caught up?" Deion asked.

"I have a guest over. I'll come up to your place and tell you all about it."

It wasn't long before she was ringing my doorbell. I was so excited. I whisked her up off the floor, turned around, and gave her a huge kiss. She was so happy. She hugged and kissed me. There's nothing like new love.

"I'm so happy to see you. You don't know how I missed you, baby," she said.

"I missed you, too. So, what's going on that I couldn't come down to your place?" he questioned.

"Well, you could have come down to my place, but I have company, so I thought we'd like a minute together alone."

"Who's your company?"

"It's Kiarra. She's staying with me for a while. She had a slight problem with her boyfriend, Derrick. She's trying to stay incognito. I thought she should come to my place so he would stop harassing her."

"Really? You mean the police officer was harassing her? I wouldn't have expected that from him." Deion uttered.

"He is a police officer but, it sounds like he's also got some issues."

"Derrick never helped her with anything he never gave her as much as a flower since their first date. She realized he wasn't the man for her. Yesterday he threw on those lights and pulled her over like he was giving her a traffic ticket. Now you know that man is crazy. Oh, and get this; he went to her neighbors and asked if she still lived there. Since she's been hiding from him.

I invited her to stay in my guest room. I'm worried about this Deion because I don't know how devious that man is. I told her she needed to go back to church because I was alone for a long time before I met you. But I prayed, and I was very specific about the man I wanted."

"I understand because 1 did the same thing, I prayed for the right woman, and then I walked in faith. It wasn't easy because I would date women, but they all wanted to have sex. I would move on because I knew she wasn't the one. Your friend is in for a difficult time if she takes the same walk we took, but her immediate priority should be to get rid of Derrick."

Dressed in a navy-blue suit, a stark white shirt, and an attractive tie, I was pleased with my appearance. I set the security alarm, locked the door, and was on my way to pick up Kosby. I rang the doorbell, and Kosby opened the door dressed in a beautiful form-fitting white dress. She had on classic black heels that showed off her sexy legs.

"I hope you don't mind, but I invited Kiarra to join us," she said sweetly.

"That's fine. Kiarra may really like my church." I said. Kiarra joined us as we left Kosby's condo.

"Why are we leaving so early?" Kosby inquired.

"It's a larger church than yours, Kosby, so we need to arrive early enough to get a good seat. Believe me, at this church; you don't want to be in the back." I explained.

"A Mega-church, I wonder if the pastor drives a Rolls-Royce or a Bentley? He probably lives in a mansion and has his very own Learjet." Kosby laughed at her own joke, then looked at me and shrugged her shoulders.

"We had good seats this morning, and a pleasant view of the Altar, the choir isn't very good, but the sermon was always on point," I whispered to Kosby.

I must admit I enjoyed the sermon, the pastor preached about how to love unlovable people. The pastor said we all run into people that we don't like. They could be family. They could be someone at the workplace, somebody we met at church, or even somebody in our community like a neighbor? He said Christ teaches us how to deal with difficult people. He asked how we could possibly be genuine with those negative emotions brawling beneath the surface level. He explained we couldn't do it on our own if we had broken sinful hearts, we were not able to deal with the flaws of our fellow man. Sometimes, we have trouble loving those nearest to us. He emphasized that the only real source of love is God. He said if we draw from him, that we could love others more sincerely. He ended his sermon by saying we should adopt an attitude of forgiveness.

"What did you think?" I asked Kosby.

"I was very impressed with the message, but the thing that bothered me was not once did he quote scripture. Now I'm very familiar with the Bible, and I'm used to my pastor backing up what he said with scripture so even though I thought it was a great sermon, it was different from the sermons that I'm used to."

We all climbed into my SUV, and I drove us over to my mother's house. We walked up to the door and rang mother's doorbell. She came to the door so excited.

"My son is here, and he brought company. I am so glad."

I hugged her and kissed her on the cheek.

"Mom, this is my girlfriend, Kosby, and this is Kosby's friend, Kiarra."

Mom smiled, and said, "Hello, thank you for coming to my home, come on in."

"You have an accent, but I can't quite make out what nationality it is?" Kosby questioned. "And you have the same amazing blue eyes as your son!"

"We are Aboriginal; we moved here three generations ago from Australia," mother replied.

"Wow, and your blonde hair is gorgeous. I'm amazed I never met anyone from Australia. I learned about the Aboriginals, but it didn't dawn on me that Deion was anything other than African American."

"Yes, and this is my grandbaby, Shantay. As you can see, she also has blue eyes and blonde hair." They were definitely a family trait, but I had black hair. Kosby seemed taken aback by seeing my family.

"Why don't you show Kosby and Kiarra the family albums," mom said.

"Yes, that's a good idea; let me get them. I'll be right back." I walked over to the couch, and I grabbed Kosby's arm.

"Come here for a minute with me. I want to talk to you." She looked at me quizzically but got up and followed me outside.

"If my mother offers you anything to eat, say you're not hungry. Our family has been here for three generations, but my mom was the first generation. I'm the second generation, and the grandkids are the third generation. My mom grew up in Australia. The Aboriginals ate from the land, which included a lot of different insects, berries, fish, and meat not eaten in America. It's like an Aboriginal trying to understand eating chitterlings and neck bones. So, if mom offers you dinner, please say no, and I will take you and Kiarra out to eat when we leave."

"I understand." Kosby said, "I'll be very polite but stern."

Kosby smiled at me, not understanding the inner turmoil I was going through. But as a child growing up in America, I was teased relentlessly when people would come over my house and find out what we ate; I just couldn't go through that.

Kosby was back in her seat next to Kiarra when my mother came back in with the photo albums. She showed pictures of my father, uncles, and many, many family members.

"Kosby, you may notice, half of the family is blonde or some variation of it from light brown to blonde, and the other half of the family has very dark hair like Deion. But one thing we all have are the prominent blue eyes." Mom explained.

Kosby asked my mother a lot of questions as she looked at the pictures. It surprised me at how interested she was. She loved to hear their names, she enjoyed looking at pictures of me growing up, and she listened to how my father died before my mother moved to America. Poor Kiarra looked bored to death. The next thing I knew, Kosby was asking my mom how she got her flowers to grow. Mama took her outside to explain her gardening secrets with Kosby as I tried to entertain Kiarra. Eventually, mom and Kosby came back. If I didn't know any better, they seemed to be best friends instead of Kosby and Kiarra.

Chapter Sixteen

Derrick

My girl had disappeared on me, and I couldn't lie. I was mad as hell. I'd been looking everywhere and couldn't find her. She hadn't been home in days. I couldn't get up to her stupid ass job because you needed to have a key card to enter. And she had the audacity to change her telephone number. On my day off I sat outside her stupid apartment in my friend's car so she wouldn't recognize it, all night long and all the next day, nothing! I've had my friends checking for her, and nobody has seen or heard from her. It was just like she disappeared off the face of the earth.

I didn't know what I'd do when I found her. Would I grab her, hug and, kiss her? Or would I attack her with my fists and knock the heck out of her? Kiarra didn't have the right to embarrass me like this! I balled up my fist and hit my hand.

I went to my bowling league. Everyone was with their women, and I was there by my damn self. She didn't know who she was messing with;

I was moving up on the list for detective. I wished I were a detective now because I'd have access to the information I couldn't get as a police officer. If I were a detective, I'd know where she was hiding. I bet she's staying at one of her bougie ass friends' houses, but I had no idea where they lived. I didn't even know their last names. But one thing I knew was that she would come back home eventually. When she came back, she'd have to deal with me because I'd be waiting for her.

She complained that I never did anything for her, so I picked out some beautiful red roses, cost me a mint I had them delivered to her simple job at the MGM however, the florist said that they could not deliver. That made me want to slap her across the face for wasting my time, my energy, and my money. Oh no, I wasn't the one. I didn't know who she had me mixed up with, one of them bozo brothers she dated in the past. But it was all good. Her day was coming. Every day I spent miserable; she'd pay double.

She obviously didn't have to work, and she didn't have to come home, so she must be sitting on a wall of dollar bills. Maybe I should have treated her a little better? Every time I thought of her, I just got angrier. I started seeing red; I wanted to hurt her. She wasn't all that.

Chapter Seventeen

Kiarra

Kosby was the very best friend a girl could ever have. We both needed to be at work at the same time, so she dropped me off at work a little earlier in the morning and picked me up from work in the evening. It was her theory that Derrick drove through that parking lot at the MGM, looking for my car. I knew she was right.

But I didn't want to wear out my welcome; I was paying rent for an apartment I couldn't even live in; it was a shame. One day Kosby and I got in Deion's car, and we drove over to my apartment, so I could get more clothes when we noticed Derrick sitting in a car a few feet down from my apartment, He was staking out the place. He didn't know Dion's car, so we just kept going.

"Unbelievable," exclaimed Kosby, "I can't understand him sitting there waiting for you to come home."

"I know I told you something was wrong with him. I tried to turn him into internal police affairs, but at this point, he hasn't done anything; so, they don't want to get involved until he kills me."

"I know, girl. It's a shame how women must protect themselves. That's why so many of us get killed every year by some crazy man."

Kosby then took me shopping and bought me a few items so I wouldn't have to keep wearing the same thing to work. I couldn't have asked for a better friend than that.

She said. "I couldn't live with myself if anything were to happen to you, and I hadn't done everything I could think of to prevent it."

My lease would be over in another month. I thought one weekend when Deion was working. I'd have Kosby take me apartment hunting. I was seriously thinking about moving to the other side of town to throw him off my scent. Maybe I could get some movers that would move me at night, so he'd still think I lived there and never be the wiser.

"I talked to one of my neighbors, and she told me he was still knocking on doors asking people if they'd seen me, and if I still lived there, everyone he asked said no," I told Kosby.

All I knew was that God blessed me with Kosby. No friend was obligated to do all the things she'd done for me. I would always love her, and maybe the time would come when I could repay the favor.

Chapter Eighteen

Kosby

My baby Deion was flying this weekend, so it was just my girl Kiarra and me. We went to Town Square, where we would meet Stacey and make a stop at Sephora and MAC cosmetics. It would be fun to do some girly things for ourselves, like buying makeup. We also planned to go to AMC to catch a movie. We made our purchases, plus they gave us a beautiful gift, compact mirrors perfect for our purses.

We left the MAC shop and headed to Sephora. Kiarra got a complete makeover by one of the sales technicians as Stacey, and I walked around looking at the makeup. She wanted to upgrade her naked collection. After her makeover, Kiarra selected a new foundation, a Naked eye collection, and a new bottle of perfume.

After leaving Sephora, we grabbed our bags and walked to the AMC theater. We walked in and looked at the movie posters to see what was playing and the times. We selected a film; Kiarra and Stacey went into the theater to get us a seat. I bought a large popcorn, two Cokes and water for Stacey. We were laughing and giggling as we left the theater when out of nowhere, we ran into Derrick.

I grabbed her hand, "We are in public he has on his uniform, which means he is on duty, and there's nothing that he can do to you right now." I said.

Kiarra uttered, "I hope you're right because he looks like a bull!"

Unfortunately, she was right. He came running towards us. I panicked, yelling and screaming, "Stacey, get out the way you're pregnant." I reached into my purse, grabbed my iPhone, and began recording him. I asked men around us to help; maybe I incited his rage because when he got to Kiarra, he immediately began to beat her. I kept screaming. I handed Stacey my phone as I tried to intervene.

"Somebody help! What's wrong with this man? What's wrong with him?" A huge crowd formed around us. It got bigger and bigger, and people enjoyed watching him beat the mess out of her until his partner got to the front and pulled that fool off my friend.

"You haven't heard the last of us, Derrick," I said, straightening my clothes. I grabbed my friend as people picked up what was left of her new cosmetics and handed them to me. Some kind man helped me get her someplace where we could sit. By this time, mall security and other police officers showed up. I told them what just transpired. "He beat this girl to a pulp." One officer was on his walkie talkie, calling for a medic. "We have an ambulance on the way. It should be here in just a moment."

The medics ran in with a gurney as the mall security cleared the area.

"She's bleeding and barely breathing," I yelled.

Another officer questioned Stacey and me while they examined Kiarra.

"What made the officer do this? She questioned.

"He's obviously crazy. Why don't you tell me why your department hired him!" I was getting sick of her stupid questions. I questioned her.

"Listen, lady, do you guys do a background check or mental health screening when you hire police officers?"

She said, "yes, ma'am, we do."

"Do you take them through any psychological examination because this man was definitely out of his mind when he went to work this morning?"

"She must have instigated this," she said.

"We were coming out of a movie. He ran up on her and began to fight her like some animal. I want you to know I will make a complaint to your department." I couldn't wait to tell my brother about this. I took footage of the entire beating. I got him from the time he ran up on us till the end when people had to pick her up off the ground.

"I will share the footage I took with every news station in Las Vegas. I will sue the Las Vegas Police Department. You guys will be lucky to be in operation next week." I told the officer. *I couldn't wait to tell my brother about this.*

As I finished talking to the officer, the medics were ready to put Kiarra into the ambulance, after scraping my friend up and onto the gurney.

"What hospital are you taking her to?" I asked. They told me, and I said I would meet them there. Stacey threw up after all the commotion; I told her to go home and rest. I called Carl and told him to watch for her since she wasn't feeling well, and he thanked me.

I drove myself over to the hospital. I found a place to park and asked for Kiarra Maxwell. They asked me if I was family and I said yes so, they took me back to her room. Doctors were working on cleaning her up and trying to address her wounds. They were prepping her to take an MRI to see if anything was broken. Kiarra was a complete mess. They told me, as they rolled her away, to have a seat, she'd be back after the MRI and CAT scan were completed.

I had a seat and called my brother on the phone.

"What's up Kosby?" he said.

"Chris you would not believe what happened today, I will send you some footage of an officer who beat Kiarra to a pulp in public today, and you will remember this man because he was at dad's retirement party sitting with Kiarra."

"I don't know, I can't believe it." he said, "Send me a copy of the footage, I want to see what happened. Let me look at it, then I'll call you right back."

"Okay, Chris."

I got on my phone and forwarded a copy of the video to my brother's email. I sat there, wringing my hands. I was so nervous I didn't know what to do. It wasn't even ten minutes before my brother called me back.

"Kosby, this is unacceptable for a police officer to do to anyone. We get a few cases where men beat up women like that at home, but most people have enough sense to know that you don't attack anybody out in public. This will be on every news station this evening, and as of this moment, that officer is suspended. I'm going to personally speak to him because Kiarra is like family to me."

"Thank you, yeah, that fool had no idea you were a Police Commander." Chris and I talked a few more minutes before he hung up. For the first time today since this horrible incident happened, I could breathe, because I knew this man would never touch her again, I hoped he got a lot of time for it too!

Chapter Nineteen

Derrick

I was on patrol with my regular partner when we got a call, a shoplifting suspect for an establishment in Town Square. We proceeded to Town Square, and when we got to the establishment, they decided not to press charges, so my partner and I left. On my way back to the car, I looked up and seen that skank Kiarra walking with her bougie friends Kosby and Stacey. They were laughing and giggling, having a good time. This girl was living the life of Riley while she had me all messed up.

Coming out of the AMC movie theatre, she looked great. I went over to talk to her, but as I got closer, she and her friends grabbed each other's hands. They all looked at me like I was the scum of the earth. All that anger that I'd been trying to control took over. I walked over to her. I couldn't say anything before I threw my first punch. It felt so good I threw another until I was beating the mess out of her. As I was beating her, I said, "oh, I'm a joke, huh, oh, you think you can hide from me. Right, oh, you don't want to see me anymore? Right well, you will remember me, yes, you will remember me." Her girlfriend Kosby was screaming and trying to jump in. Her pleas fell on deaf ears because nobody wanted to get mixed up with whatever was going on. But somehow, I knew there was a group of people around us. I thought, oh no, they're taking videos, I'm going to end up in trouble. But I looked at her again, and I kept punching. Next thing I knew, my partner was pulling me off this woman saying, "come on man, are you crazy?" Suddenly my mind came back to me. I realized what had I done, and I knew I was in trouble.

My partner walked me back to the car. We got in and drove to the station.

"Come on, man, you know there will be some rebuttal for what you did to that lady today."

"I know, man. I don't understand what happened to me. I just lost it." I found a seat. I sat there in a stupor.

My Sergeant came out of the office.

"Go back on patrol alone," he told my partner, who left immediately. I knew he didn't want any trouble.

He then looked at me disgusted and said,

"You sit here and don't move. I was summoned to the Commander's office."

I don't know how long I sat there, but it felt like forever. It appeared time was moving so slow. The reality of what happened kicked in, and I knew I might have jeopardized my position with the police department. I noticed officers coming in and going out, none of them spoke to me; they just looked at me pitifully. But even their looks couldn't compare to the way I felt at that moment. I was that little boy who grew up in the hood, who stayed out of trouble and got on with the police department. My old friends in the hood were so proud. My mother told everyone her son was a police officer, and at reunions, the whole family was proud of me. I couldn't believe I let some trick mess me up so bad that I'd probably lose my job. I wanted to cry, but I was a man. I had to face my realities like a grown-up. The way the Sergeant told me to stay seated in that spot, I felt like I was in timeout. I got up and went to the bathroom. When I got in the stall, I cried; I cried like a baby.

What was I going to do now? I didn't go to college. I didn't know how I would support myself if I lost this job. Anger hit me all over again. If I lost this job over that trick, she'd really have to pay. I walked over to the sink, grabbed some paper towels, wet them, and washed my face. I went back and sat exactly where the Sergeant told me to stay. After what felt like hours, the Sergeant came back. He called me into his office. I was told to have a seat.

"Man, what were you thinking? Why would you attack that lady in public as an animal?

I looked at the Sergeant. "I need to talk to my union representative; until informed of my rights, I don't want to make any statements."

"No problem. You will have a chance to talk to your union representative. You'll also be talking to internal affairs, and right now, you're officially on paid suspension until we can unravel this situation." My Sergeant looked at me. "Off the record, did you know that the friend of the lady you beat today is our Commander's sister? He told me he saw you with that lady you beat up at his father's retirement party. His father was a pilot. Do you remember that?"

I put my head down in my hands. How would I know that our Commander was Kiarra's bougie girlfriend, Kosby's brother? I now know I've lost my job.

"What do I need to do before I leave? I asked.

"You need to give me your gun, your badge, and your police identification. You should also clean out your locker until you have time to talk with your union representative and internal affairs. That's all. You are dismissed."

I grabbed a tote to clean out my locker. All I felt was rage. If he hadn't taken my firearm, I would've shot him and every police officer in this place. I tried to calm myself down. My temper was the reason I was in this situation right now. I wondered how Kiarra was doing. I hope I didn't hurt her too severely because her next move was to sue the police department. With Kosby as an eyewitness, she'd win a mint from the city and my job, too!

With all my things in tow, I headed for my car. I drove home, obeying all the safety laws. Once I got home, dropped the tote on the floor, poured a glass of Jack Daniels, and added some ice cubes, I sat down and drank it straight. I grabbed the remote, flipped on the TV, and much to my horror, I see myself running over to Kiarra; my face was unfamiliar. The menacing look I wore scared me. I approached her and proceeded to beat her ruthlessly, throwing punch after punch like I was a champ fighting for a million-dollar purse. I was in shock. They had reporters over at Town Square asking people who were standing by what they saw. Their descriptions of my attack were gruesome. I knew I was in trouble because my story was at the top of the news. I flipped through the channels. I was on every local station.

I realized my mother knew, my family knew, everyone I grew up with knew. I was defeated. I couldn't understand why I let that one chick get on my nerves so bad. Truthfully, I wished she had never been born.

Chapter Twenty

Kosby

"Are you the relative of Kiarra Maxwell?"

"Yes, I am."

"Kiarra's had an MRI, CT scan, and examination by the doctor. They have admitted her. She is in ICU. Don't be alarmed, but the doctor ordered 24-hour surveillance. It's just a precaution because she was hit on the head so many times. They will wake her up every two hours to make sure she's okay. Visiting hours in ICU differ from the rest of the hospital. Two family members can visit her at any hour of the day or night. There is a waiting room attached to the ICU. You must turn your ringer off on your cell phone; you can make and take calls in there. You may be asked to leave ICU when doctors are doing examinations. You can wait in the waiting room. The staff will come and inform you when you can go back in. Do you have any questions?"

"What is her diagnosis?"

"The doctor will answer those questions for you, and the staff will keep you informed of everything that is going on. You can follow me."

This was the first time I'd ever seen an

ICU unit. She took me into Kiarra's room; she was sleeping. I sat down in the chair. I felt a tear come to my eye, then another one, and before I knew it, I was crying. I got up and grabbed a Kleenex. I tried to straighten myself up. I pulled my chair closer to her bed, and I held her hand.

"Kiarra, you're my best friend, and I love you so much, so please pull through this. I promise to take care of you until you're able to take care of yourself again."

I held her hand and sat there until the doctor came in. He walked up to me, introduced himself, and I introduced myself.

"Let's go into the waiting room, and I'll tell you what's going on with Kiarra." Together we walked over to the waiting room.

"She suffered multiple blows to her head, causing several contusions; she also had several breaks. The worst thing is the fact that he hit her in the eye. Tomorrow you will see a black eye, he fractured her face, but there's nothing we can do to fix that. Now for the breaks, her foot has a hairline fracture on the left, the right ankle has a break. The orthopedic surgeon will get her ready in the morning for surgery because she also has a fractured rib. Now that fracture is extremely dangerous because if she were to move the wrong way, it could either puncture her heart or her lungs. We have her on pain medication to help keep her comfortable. But because of the contusions, we must wake her up every two hours, so we're unable to give her any heavy-duty pain medication. Do you have any questions?"

"That's a lot to take in, no, not at this time," I answered.

He led me back to her room, and I resumed my spot in the chair, holding her hand. It was a long evening as the nurses came and went. Different staff was coming in to check this or that. Someone came several times to take blood, residents, doctors, and nurses; every one of them came and went. They monitored her; I felt so sorry for her because her face was so swollen and bruised. She couldn't get any rest because they woke her up every two hours, making her answer questions to ensure she was okay because of the head injuries.

I went into the waiting area and called Deion. I figured he'd be at his hotel by now he answered, "Hey baby, how are you doing?"

I said, "not so good," before I could tell him what had transpired today.

"I know Kiarra is in the hospital. I saw Derrick beat her to a pulp on the news."

"Oh, my goodness, you saw that on your local news in New York?"

"Yes, it's probably a nationwide story because it was so brutal. Had I realized Derrick was that crazy, I would have told you guys to not leave your condo without me. But who in their right mind would ever think you wouldn't be safe in a public forum to go shopping and watch a movie?"

"I know sweetie, it's mind-boggling. I tell you the minute I saw him I knew he was coming for her. I was asking people for help, but no one would step up to help, I can't believe people! I tried to intervene; he was just too strong for me. After his partner finally came over there and got him off Kiarra, someone came over to help me get her to a seat."

"I'm just glad you weren't hurt trying to help her. There is already too much violence in the world without police officers treating citizens like that. Who would have ever thought the man was so crazy?" he said.

"She tried to tell us; she insisted he was stalking her, and that's why I had her move in with me. Baby, you should see her face. It's so swollen up; it's cut and bruised, and she has a black eye. She has surgery in the morning for a broken rib. I have been sitting here praying. I don't know what to do. I decided I would stay here with her throughout this surgery, and I would wait for her to get well enough to talk to me. In the meantime, I'll be taking time off work," I explained.

"Okay, hey, I should be back into Vegas tomorrow evening. As soon as I get there, I'll come straight to the hospital to join you. Of course, you know you can call me or text me anytime you need to."

"I know, Deion, and I appreciate you so much. No worries, I got this. I tell you Derrick will be the one sorry that he ever met Kiarra."

We said our goodbyes and hung up. I got a Coke because I was exhausted, but I would stay in her room all night long.

I dozed off in that chair several times. I was just exhausted, but like clockwork every two hours, they came in to wake her up; me being in the room, it also woke me up. Her surgery was scheduled early in the morning, and soon as she went into surgery, I would run home, take a shower, and put on some clean clothes.

They finally came to take her to the operating room, so I took the opportunity to go home and get myself cleaned up. Although the shower helped, I was still tired. I returned to her room, but she hadn't made it out of surgery yet.

"Her surgeries went well; they were able to mend her rib. Kiarra is now in recovery; it will be awhile before she wakes up. We will bring her back to ICU and monitor her another day. If she continues to do well, we will move her into a regular room," one of the residents saw me and said.

I thanked the doctor for the information. I shook his hand, and he left. I went to the lounge to get a cup of coffee and called my mom and dad. We discussed the horrible tragedy. Mom asked me to let them know as soon as they moved her to a regular room, so they could come to visit her. After I hung up with them, I talked to Stacey. I noticed she tried calling me several times. I explained to her how I had to turn off my phone while in the ICU.

She apologized for not being there but explained that her morning sickness had been pretty bad. I didn't complain to Stacey that I had been up for an entire day and needed to lie down and get some sleep. We said our goodbye's and got off the telephone. I sat in that chair and went to sleep until they returned Kiarra to the room.

Chapter Twenty-One

Deion

As we taxied away from the runway, we raised the flaps and reset the flight controls. I was excited to get back home as we landed at McCarran Airport. We had a perfect landing, and the ramp personnel got on board to do their jobs.

I hopped onboard the employee shuttle that took me to the employee parking lot. I grabbed my suitcase and made my way to my car. I put the bag in the trunk because I was on my way to the hospital, so I could see my baby Kosby and check on Kiarra.

As I stepped off the elevator at ICU, I walked into the room. Kosby and Kiarra were talking. Kosby looked up, ran over, hugged, and kissed me. I reciprocated until I remembered where I was. I looked over at Kiarra,

"Hey, how are you doing?"

"I know I look awful, but I'm grateful to God that I'm still here," she said.

"Yes, I am so happy you made it through all of this. I felt so guilty that I wasn't with you two when you ran into that fool.

Kiarra said, "No, there's no need for you to

feel guilty because I had figured out a long time ago that Derrick was psycho. I told Kosby, and like any good friend, she did her best to get me away from that maniac. But Vegas is a small town, and the way I see it, he would have eventually found me. But even I never imagined he would have turned out to be as crazy as he was."

Kiarra's words sounded so painful. She needed to save her strength and concentrate on getting well. I grabbed the second chair next to Kosby and had a seat.

I asked Kiarra, "Have your parents been up here to visit you?"

"No, I hadn't seen my father since I was three years old when he left the family. My mother worked two jobs for years until she worked herself to death. I have three siblings, two brothers and a sister, and as soon as they turned 18 years old, they all left Las Vegas, respectively, and we're not good about keeping in touch."

"Wow," I said. "That was the wrong question to ask. No wonder Kosby feels like she's your family, because she is."

"It's okay, Deion; I've come to grips with Kosby and Stacey being my family."

Kosby grabbed my hand. She must've seen how uncomfortable this conversation was for me.

"I need a cup of coffee. Would either of you

like anything?" They both declined, so I got up and found the waiting room because there was a coffee station in there. I made myself a cup and had a seat in a chair while I watched television. Ready to go home; it had been a long day for me. I worked all day, and now I had to sit at this hospital. I prayed a lot because I tended to be on the selfish side, and I knew it. When it's our motivation to make it in this world, it was good for us to be a little selfish. Like anything, you could take it too far, and that's when I had to pray.

"Hey, sweetie," she said as she joined me on the couch.

"My mother and father came to visit. There can only be two people in ICU, so it gave me a chance to see my favorite sweetie.

"So, you have other sweetie's," I ask her jokingly.

"Well, I do have other sweetie's, but I don't feel the same way about any of them as I feel about you."

A little taken back, I wondered if she was telling me she sees other men? Did I take it for granted that we were exclusive? Disturbed, I questioned, "So does that mean you're dating other men?"

She chuckled. "No, of course not. You know how I feel about you. I'm referring to other people in my life, like my mom, and dad, my brother, and my friends. I consider all of them to be my sweetie's, but I consider you to be my love."

Wow, that shocked me. I hadn't expected Kosby to say she loved me. I had been trying for a long time to let her know that she was the love of my life, but she's the one who said it first.

I stood up, grabbed her hand. She stood up with me. We kissed, and at that moment in time, there was no one on this earth except Kosby and me. As soon as we finished, someone walked into the room, so we sat back down. She laid her head on my shoulder. No matter what I go through in this life, I was sure this was a moment I would always fondly remember.

Chapter Twenty-Two

Kosby

I missed church on Sunday and two days of work before returning, after the tragedy with Kiarra. It felt good to get back to work because I had something else to concentrate on rather than the injustice she suffered. All morning, people were coming by my office welcoming me back, as if something had happened to me, well, I guess it did. I was fortunate because my boss was very understanding, but he told me we had to get this work done.

Sean, my boss, said, "If it means working overtime or taking it home in the evening, whatever you need to do to catch up because this place operates based on the numbers you give us."

"No problem," I promised. "I'll get the work done and get it to you ASAP."

I'd been working hard today trying to catch up with two days of work, and because of today's work, it's the third day. It wouldn't have been so bad, but the person who did my job in my absence was on vacation. I sat there with my pens, papers, pencils, erasers, calculator, my computer, and everything I needed to come up with the proper calculations. I found something interesting when I did several days at a time. The calculations were clear to me. I was able to get caught up that day. I skipped taking a break and lunch, but I had my report ready and on Sean's desk before I went home that evening.

After work, I went home. Deion was flying, and Kiarra was in a regular room mending at the hospital. I went straight home to my bedroom to lie down on the bed, and I went straight to sleep.

When I woke up, I realized it was too late for me to go to the hospital to see Kiarra. I was so tired, and it had been so long since I slept all night in a real bed. Going back to work today and playing catch up was taxing on me. I just needed some rest. I called Kiarra on the phone to tell her I was sorry I didn't make it this evening but, of course, my girl was so sweet.

"Don't worry, you've been here the entire time," she said.

I got up, put my nightclothes on, and went to bed. I needed some good sleep.

I woke up early the next morning refreshed for the first time in about a week. I took a much-needed shower. I enjoyed standing under the rain shower head. I got out, dried off, added lotion on my body, put hair products in my natural hair, and dressed for work. I got there early, sat down, had a cup of coffee, and looked at the information on my desk to start a new day.

Sean came to my office. "Kiarra, you did an excellent job on that report yesterday. It was so phenomenal the bigwigs are all humming about it this morning." he beamed.

I smiled at Sean, "Thank you, I know I did it, but I prayed to get caught up on that work, and it just seemed to happen the way it was supposed to happen."

"Whatever it takes," he replied.

Sean left my office, and I started working on today's actuary report. Because I was caught up with my work, I decided today would be the day that I had the luxury of having lunch, so I ordered a nice salad and some iced tea.

After work, I went to the hospital to visit Kiarra. She looked somewhat better, but that black eye was a shiner.

I smiled. "How's my friend doing today?"

"Oh, actually, it's been pretty good. I'm feeling a lot better; of course, I'm sore. Your brother Chris came by to see me today. I thought that was sweet of him. He told me that Derrick had a hearing coming up, and he assured me if he had anything to do with it, Derrick would be looking for a new job. He also told me that soon as I could get out of this Hospital, I should find myself a lawyer and sue the City because Derrick was on duty. That footage Stacey captured on your phone went viral nationwide. He told me not to tell anyone except you that he put the thought in my head to sue."

"Yeah, my brother is a charmer. Suing had always been on my mind. We will find the best lawyer in Las Vegas and girl, they'll probably settle with you, but regardless your health is most important. You can move out of that apartment and buy yourself a nice house and live on easy street. My advice to you is to pay cash so you won't have a mortgage, all you'll have to pay is your taxes and insurance every year, and you'll have money to do all the things you've always wanted to do. You can travel, buy new furniture and fix your place up any way you want. Too bad you had to pay for it by getting beat to a pulp. Now it's Derrick's responsibility to pay. He'll be sorry he ever laid hands on any woman. He'll be without a job, without job possibilities and money. I wonder, was it worth all that?"

For the first time in over a week, Kiarra laughed.

"Kosby, you just made my day."

I smiled. "Well, you make my day every day." I grabbed her hand.

Her room looked lovely with all the bouquets she had received from me, my parents, Chris, Stacey, and her co-workers even sent her flowers. Each bouquet was stunning.

"See how many people love you?"

"Yes, I hadn't realized that that many people cared."

After visiting for a while, the nurse came in to tell me visiting hours were over. I was thankful because I was ready to go home. I bent down and gave her a peck on her forehead. I left the room and headed home.

Grabbing food from a fast-food restaurant because it was too late to cook dinner, I took it home, turned on the television, and joyfully watched a show while eating my food in peace. I called my baby on the phone. He told me he just walked into his hotel room.

"Kosby, I am so happy to hear from you. I thought about you all day long, you know I'm looking forward to coming home, and I'll be there tomorrow evening."

"I'm looking forward to seeing you too, sweetheart, I'll do my best to cook you a nice home-cooked meal tomorrow. You deserve that after all, you've been through." I offered.

He said, "See, that's why I love you. You're just so thoughtful."

"I am very blessed," I said.

We continued to chat about his day, my day, and I brought him up to date on Kiarra. We ended the conversation with lots of love and kisses through the phone.

Even though I had fast food, I cleaned up my dishes and threw all the bags in the trash; I took the garbage out and put in a new liner. I washed my face thoroughly, put on my night moisturizer, nightgown, and I believe I was asleep even before my head hit the pillow.

Chapter Twenty-Three

Derrick

I had been sitting at home ever since I went berserk and beat up Kiarra. My phone rang all the time. I looked down to see who it was; because I didn't want to talk to anybody except the police department. I spoke to my union steward, who told me that things weren't looking good for me.

"Why would you attack that lady?" He asked me. That was the million-dollar question everyone kept asking, including myself.

"I don't even have a good answer. She disrespected me, and when I saw her, I felt she needed to pay for all the disrespect she gave me," I said.

"We don't have a good defense. Once internal affairs calls you in to talk with them, you need to tell them something that makes sense as to why you attacked that woman! The Commander is asking for your immediate dismissal. Fortunately, the department isn't set up that way. Even he doesn't have the power to do that to you. But if you can't come up with a logical reason as to why you attacked that young lady, then you may as well kiss your position with the police department goodbye."

I realized I had no logical reason for attacking her, so I sat there drinking, trying to drown myself, avoiding personal calls. I didn't want to hear my mama whining, because I helped her with bills. I didn't want any of those folks from back in the day saying we knew you couldn't handle that job man I don't even know why you tried.

But my greatest fear was that I'd have to go to jail. With all the criminals I mistreated, I'd probably get my butt kicked for breakfast, lunch, and dinner. I thought about killing myself, but that wasn't a viable solution. I know when I got the money from my retirement fund, I was moving out of this city someplace where nobody knew me. Although, that might be hard to do if I stay in America because that footage went viral. I took another drink and realized my glass was empty, so I got up and made myself another one; I only had half a glass because the bottle was empty. I filled it up with ice and sat here and drank some more until I passed out.

When I woke up, I had one hell of a hangover. I felt so bad I got up to look for some aspirin. I grabbed a bottle of water and drank it to wash the aspirin down but soon as I got it down, I threw it all back up. I moaned in my awful situation. Hard to believe this time last year, I had a beautiful life. I was on top of the world, I had a job I loved, and people respected me. I had a good partner with the Police Department, and now I was despised.

Once I could pull myself off the ground, I got in the shower washed my face. Brushed that nasty taste out of my mouth and put on some clean clothes. My apartment was a mess, just like my life. I decided it was time for me to straighten up my life. The first step was to clean this apartment. I gathered all my clothes sat them in front of the washer to separate them by color. I put in the load, and one by one, I repeated the process. In the meantime, I cleaned my tub, the shower, I washed the toilet, and I washed the sinks. Then I removed the sheets from my bed. I threw them in the stack of dirty laundry. I vacuum the room, open the windows to get the stench out. After putting on a new set of sheets, I made up my bed and started on the kitchen. I wiped down the counter, swept the floor, mopped the kitchen, and headed to the living room area. This was my worst room. I grabbed a big black trash bag and stuffed fast-food wrappers and newspapers into the bag that I never wanted to read again. I opened more windows to let fresh air in. I was sick of the stench. I pulled the couch apart and vacuumed the pillows put the couch back together, and vacuumed the floor. I sprayed Windex on my end tables and cocktail table I wiped and wiped until tears were pouring out of my eyes. I laid my head in my hands, not sure what I would do.

I called a lawyer I knew was one of the best. I made an appointment to talk to him about my dilemma, and for the first time, I feel like maybe I could save myself and keep my life.

Chapter Twenty-Four

Deion

I had a nice flight, but it was always good to get back home to see my lady, I was so fortunate to have Kosby. I went straight to my apartment, separated my clothes that needed to go to the cleaners, and put my dirty clothes in the hamper. I took a quick shower, got dressed, and called my girl on the phone.

She was thrilled to hear my voice and told me to come on down. She cooked me a nice dinner. So, I grabbed my keys, got on the elevator rode two floors down. She opened the door, looking lovely as ever, and invited me in. I knew she showed up and showed out because the scent of tasty food drifted through the air.

"Would you like a drink? she asked me."

"Yes, I answered. I'll take a Heineken."

"Oh, you'll be happy to see Kiarra. She looks so much better, and she's getting out of the hospital tomorrow."

"That's great," I say. "I know Kiarra's ready

to come home. I couldn't believe all she's gone through. Do you think she'll be up to going to church with us on Sunday?"

"I doubt it. She's on crutches and bed rest. Although her face looks better, it's still puffy and swollen. Thanks to her yellow skin, that black eye is still prominent."

"Well, at least at home with the crutches, she'll be able to get around the apartment and not have to worry about anybody bothering her."

"I know, but I thought I'd let her come stay here at least for a few days until she gets accustomed to getting around on the crutches. I am so excited about us going to my church on Sunday," Kosby commented.

"Who said we were going to your church. I thought we could go back to mine?" I questioned.

"We haven't settled whose church we would be attending, by the way, that's something we need to sit down and discuss. My church is much smaller than yours, and everyone is friendly; they know you by name, and we do a lot of activities together. I thought we could join my church." she said.

"Well, actually, I enjoy my Pastor. I love the way he preaches the word, and even though it's a megachurch and they may not know you personally, the service is always right on point," I countered.

"Are you trying to say that my Pastor is not as good at preaching? Because the way I see it, my Pastor quotes scripture and explains it, whereas your Pastor gets up and talks, but not once did he quote one scripture out of the Bible."

"Kosby, can we just agree to disagree. Since I'm the man in this relationship, I should be the one to make the final decision, and I say we go to my church."

"Sweetie, we are in the 21st Century. Relationships are no longer one-sided, together we are partners. We make decisions together. Your vote is no bigger than my vote. The way I see it, we're 50/50. Now we can compromise, or you can go to your church, and I'll continue to go to my church."

"What kind of compromising are you talking about, Kosby?"

"Since we went to your church last time, why don't we go to my church this time and then the next time we'll go back to your church, now how's that for compromising?" she asked.

"Honestly, it seems silly for us to be splitting our time between two churches when our relationship is built on God, so we ought to be adult enough to go to the teaching church which is mine, rather than the Pastor screaming at church, which is yours," I said.

"Say what? You think my Pastor was screaming at the church, oh I forgot you weren't raised as an Afro American, your roots are Aboriginal. Tell me what kind of church you attended in Australia." Kosby said vindictively.

"Don't get childish Kosby; you know that I was raised in America. I'm every bit as American as you are. You know what? I've suddenly lost my appetite. We can both go to our own churches on Sunday!" I got up and walked out the door, leaving Kosby standing there with her mouth open.

Chapter Twenty-Five

Kosby

I couldn't figure out what just happened. Deion and I always got along perfectly, yet out of the blue, we argued over whose church we'd attend. This was so ridiculous. I had no idea something this trivial would break us up. He must have been looking for any reason to break up with me because that was not the Deion I knew.

I went back into the kitchen to finish getting my meal together; I had dinner alone with lots of leftovers. I put the leftovers in Tupperware and stored them in the refrigerator. I cleaned the kitchen and turned off the TV. In my room, I sat and wondered if Derrick were this mad when he attacked my friend Kiarra.

I washed and moisturized my face, put on my nightgown, and got in the bed. I felt like I had been in a car accident. I hurt so bad because I never saw this coming. I thought I had met my soulmate. I guess I was out of line when I told him he wasn't American because he was born in this country just like I was. Geez, how do you know when something so perfect, so beautiful could turn left?

I lie in my bed, it was early, and I wasn't sleepy, but I keep replaying tonight over and over in my head. I felt the tears well up in my eyes. I thought about getting dressed and going to him to apologize and letting him know I'd go to his church. But I decided not to. Because if I did that would set the precedent for the rest of our relationship. He'd always be right, I'd always be apologizing, and he would always get his way. I refused to be in a relationship like that. I got up and grabbed a Lime-a-Rita. I enjoyed the drink while I listened to some smooth jazz.

If Deion was that petty, I was glad I found out now! He was so selfish he wasn't even able to compromise, which showed me he didn't love me the way I thought he did. I finished my drink, turned off the music, and went back to bed. This time I slept until morning.

I got up bright and early, took a shower under the regular nozzle, and went through my daily routine to get ready for work. I checked the time I realized I needed to leave for work, so I set the alarm, locked the door, and hopped on the elevator. I got into my car, and on my way, I stopped for an impromptu Grande Cappuccino from Starbucks.

I got on the elevator and proceeded to my office. I grabbed my work for the day and began making my calculations. I worked hard because I didn't want to even think about my personal life at that moment. I worked so hard until I realized I hadn't had anything to eat all day, so I left for lunch. I ordered a nice BLT sandwich, fries, and a Coca-Cola. After I finished my lunch, I went back to work to complete my calculations. When my workday was over, I hopped in my car and drove to the hospital to pick up Kiarra. She was so happy to see me; she was packed sitting on the bed, ready to go. I walked up to her and gave her a big hug. I grabbed her things.

"What do you need to do to get checked out?" I questioned.

"We can tell the nurse on the way out because I've already signed all the papers."

We stop by the nurse's station, and the nurse comes around with a wheelchair.

"It's hospital rules that we take the patient out in a wheelchair and load them into their car."

"No problem." We got on the elevator and went to the first floor.

"Let me go get my car, I'll pull it around, and you can load her in."

Once we got home, I unloaded her, got her on the elevator and to my condo. I sat her on the couch, locked my front door, and turned on the alarm.

"I'm surprised Deion isn't with you."

I forced a smile, "We broke up last night."

"Seriously, you two were the perfect couple. What happened?"

I told her about our fight how I refused to

give in because he'd act that way the rest of our relationship if I did. Kiarra agreed with me.

"Kosby, we all have faults and flaws in our personalities. He just showed you his. He was selfish; it was his way or no way! Just give him a few days to realize he was wrong. If he doesn't, you are better off without him. I saw Derrick's red flags and ignored them until I couldn't take them anymore. He was such a chauvinist he couldn't get over the fact that I left him. If he had met someone he liked more, he wouldn't have had a problem telling me to kick rocks, and he would have never bothered me."

I sat there and thought about what she said. I knew she was right, my parents had flaws, but they could cope with each other's idiosyncrasies. I didn't want a relationship where I was always apologizing, and he had everything his way. Best to see it now, that's why I adored my girls because they were the epitome of reason.

Chapter Twenty-Six

Deion

I went to church and tried to enjoy the service, but my mind was on Kosby. I couldn't even hear the service because I was contemplating why I was here alone. Why was I so stubborn when she offered a solution, but I wouldn't have it? I said no, we either go to my church or no church. I may as well have said we either do it my way because you don't have any say in this relationship. I didn't understand what made me act that way. When they had the call to the altar, I went up and got on my knees, and I prayed, I asked God to help me be a better person. I asked him to help me be more reasonable and to please help me get my girlfriend Kosby back. After church, I went over my mom's house. I told her what happened.

"Kosby cooked me a nice dinner the other night."

Mom said, "That's wonderful."

"I don't know because we never got that far, I brought up the subject of going to church on Sunday, so I said let's go to my church. Kosby said we went to your church last time, and we haven't discussed who's church we would attend. But mom, all I could think about was I like my church, and I decided that that's where Kosby and I would attend.

Kosby offered a compromise by going to my church one week and her church one week until we decided which church, we enjoyed going to the best.

I was unyielding, and we broke up. I didn't want to compromise. I heard nothing unless she would come to my church and join. So, we broke up. I didn't get my good dinner either; I left feeling salty."

"You hadn't changed a bit when you were a child you were very selfish, I used to tell you, you were selfish, and you're still selfish that's why you could not compromise because it's your way or no way. I think she would make you a good wife one day, so son, you need to be a man, and you need to rectify the situation. You should tell Kosby after thinking about it you realized that a compromise would settle the argument for now and after you're more comfortable with each other's church, you can sit down and talk about it intelligently."

"You're right, Mom. Emotions motivated me. I couldn't understand Kosby not thinking the same thing I thought because she and I already think so much alike we can finish each other's sentences. We always got along so well, we never fought, so it was such a surprise when we weren't in agreement. At that moment in time, I thought the only way I could prove I was the man was by insisting that she attend my church. Today, she went to her church, and I went to mine, today she's eating with her family, and I'm over here eating with my family. We'll keep going our separate ways until we forget we ever knew each other. Once too much time has passed it'll be too late to ever reconcile."

Mom said, "Yeah, that's right; she sees you as a spoiled, selfish young man, and all the points you scored with her went right out the window. So now you need to stand up and be a man, or you need to move on with your life and forget her, it's your decision."

We changed the subject. I had an enjoyable lunch with my mother. Mom went outside to the garden while I turned on the game. I sat around, not wanting to go home. I hadn't slept well since I had that argument with Kosby. I must've fallen asleep on the couch because I woke up under a blanket, and mother was watching some silly show. I looked out the window; it was dark. "Mom, how long have I been asleep?"

"It must have been some time honey because your game went off and I've been watching the television. I figured you were exhausted, or you wouldn't have slept like that. It's good to get sleep when you fly an airplane every day."

"You are so funny; let's take a trip somewhere.

You know you have benefits; you can fly anywhere." I reminded mom.

"Yes, I know, and I've used them, but I like it here. I like to be here when the kids come to visit me and the grandkids; that's what I enjoy."

I said, "Mom, how about one day you and I go back to the old country, back to Australia so you can see your old friends that still live there. Don't you think that would be a nice trip?"

"Yes, that would be a wonderful trip. I have plenty of family that still lives there. It would be so much fun; it would feel like a reunion for me. We should decide on a time and take that trip together."

I got up, stretched, bent over, and kissed mom on the cheek. I said, "Figure out what week you are not babysitting or what week you want to go, I'll take time off work we'll do this, it'll be a lot of fun."

Mom said, "Yes, it will be a lot of fun."

I folded up the blanket she had laid across me. I sat it on the couch and grabbed my keys. I thanked mom for such a beautiful day. I went home, and I got ready for bed even though I had slept a long time I realized being angry and upset would only cause another restless night. I wasn't getting the correct amount of sleep, and I had to work tomorrow. I'd call Kosby when I got back from this trip.

Chapter Twenty-Seven

Kiarra

I called Chris and asked him to give me the name of the very best lawyer in town. He recommended Ronald Sanders, and I thanked him. I called Ronald Sander's office and made an appointment with him. I got an appointment the very next day at three p.m. With that complete, I fixed Kosby a nice dinner because she and her family were always wonderful to me. I looked in the refrigerator and found some pork chops. I pulled them out so they could thaw out that way I could have dinner ready when she got home. I went to my room and decided on a navy-blue suit to wear to the lawyer's office tomorrow. I went back into the living room, turned on some music. Oh yeah, I liked those oldies. Starting to feel like my old self, I sang my heart out with the song.

I grilled the pork chops, made mashed potatoes along with some Italian green beans, and to top it off; I made her my signature crescent rolls from scratch. I heard Kosby walk in the door.

"Oh, my goodness, it smells amazing in here, what did you cook?"

After sharing my menu, I said. "I would have made you something fancy, but, with both my feet broken, I couldn't drive to the store."

"I'm just excited because I'm so used to cooking all my own meals. Let me change out of my work clothes and wash my hands; then we can sit down, have dinner, and talk." We sat down to eat.

"I called Chris to get a referral, I made an appointment to see a lawyer tomorrow," she said.

"That's great. Now my question is, how are you going to get to the lawyer's office knowing that I work, and I overstayed my time off?"

I smiled at her and said, "You think you have to do everything; you believe you have to be the perfect girl? No, that's why they have Uber and Lyft to pick people up who can't drive."

She laughed and said, "Ahhh, I got my old Kiarra back. My girl is independent and can handle business. I'm happy that you're taking these steps to take back everything he tried to take from you."

I smiled at her. "No worries if I could raise all my mother's kids, fix dinner, fix breakfast, go to school and still be on the Dean's List, there is no way that some stupid ass, excuse my French police officer is going ever to get the best of me."

"That's my girl, why don't you make a list and I'll go to the grocery store, and we can take turns making each other dinner," Kosby suggested.

"Okay, I'll do that after dinner. We finished our dinner with an inspiring conversation.

The next day as soon as Kosby had gone to work, I put plastic bags around my casts and tied them up with rubber bands. I hopped in the shower to clean myself up and wash my hair. Being on crutches, I wasn't up to doing much to my hair, so I pulled it back in a neat little bun. After I finished with my hair, I got dressed in my suit; now it was time for a ride. I had the Lyft app on my telephone; it told me a driver would pick me up in four minutes in the parking lot. I got off the elevator at the garage level when I heard my phone ding telling me my Lyft driver was here. It said his name was Eric and he was driving a BMW I looked up, and I saw the BMW sitting right in front of me.

"Are you, Eric?

"Yes." He helped me to get in the car with my crutches. He asked me where I was going. I confirmed the address of the lawyer's office. I sat back and scrolled through my telephone, thinking how much real life I had missed. He got me to my destination in no time, and the price was very reasonable. With my crutches, I hopped my way to the elevator and into the attorney's suite. After I struggled to get the door open and made it to the front desk, the receptionist greeted me.

"Hi, may I help you?"

I said, "Yes, I'm here to see Ronald Sander's."

"Please have a seat. He'll be with you in one moment." Once I was called in and seated in the attorney's office. I gave him the rundown.

"I'm familiar with your case. I've seen it on TV."

"Well, I guess I'm just a regular star like Rodney King." I joked.

That must have struck his funny bone because he laughed.

"We have several directions we can go with your case; the first one would be to sue the City because that police officer was on active duty when he attacked you. We will also sue that police officer in civil court to make him responsible for his actions. The City will most likely prosecute him for assault."

This lawyer sounded like he knew what he was talking about; he was very descriptive; he took his time explaining things to me. He told me why we were doing some of the litigation one way. He also explained why we were doing the other parts of the case another way.

"You will win this case. My fees are high, but I talked to Commander Matthews, and I'll handle both of your cases at a fraction of my normal price because I could also use the exposure that you will get when you win this case. The news will be national."

We finished our business and shook hands. He helped me out to the lobby. When I got to the lobby, I called Lyft; they let me know a driver would be here in five minutes.

Chapter Twenty-Eight

Derrick

I wanted to drink. I couldn't believe how much I wanted to drink. Just when I thought I had the strength to make it, I got hit with more bull crap- served with a subpoena for civil court. Kiarra was suing me. Today I have a hearing with my union steward and internal affairs. If that's not enough, my lawyer told me not to take any of my pension money out because if I converted it out of the pension and lose my civil case with Kiarra, she could collect every dime I had. I don't know who or what could help me in this hour of need, but I was in the worst situation I'd ever endured in my entire life.

I hadn't had a drink in several days. I wanted to be presentable for my afternoon meeting. I took a shower, making it so hot I wished my skin would fall off. After I got out and dried off, I put on a nice suit. My shoes were nice and shiny. I was clean; my eyes were white, and I didn't smell like alcohol. I headed to the station for my meeting.

I arrived at the station early just as my union steward instructed. I met him, where he briefed me on what would happen. He escorted me to the internal affairs hearing room, and we had a seat outside while we waited for them to call us in. My union steward told me not to be nervous but to be clear and concise; when I asked questions, he explained the different things that could happen.

I know he was trying his best not to make me nervous about this, but the department never had an incident this severe before. I sat there and waited for them to call us in. It wasn't long before an officer came out and asked us to come in. He then instructed us where to sit. It was a huge conference table. There was a screen on the front wall TV monitor on the side; there were microphones at each of the respective seats. Once we were seated, I noticed the police entered the room according to rank importance from lowest to highest, first, the Police Sergeant came in, then the Lieutenant, the Internal Affairs Lieutenant, the Commander, the Deputy Chief and finally the Chief of Police.

I knew I was in trouble when I saw the Chief of Police walk in. He didn't attend anything unless it's super important. My heart dropped. I didn't even know if I'd be able to talk in front of these people without breaking down crying like a little boy. Still, I hadn't understood what happened to me.

The Lieutenant said, "the charges against officer Andrews are excessive force, police brutality, and misconduct of a police officer. We find if Officer Andrews is guilty, his charges can range from verbal counseling to termination. For the record, I'd like to say that Internal Affairs only becomes involved if there is a citizen complaint or Command determines that an incident should be investigated. Command sent a copy of a video, which was sent to him by a citizen. As a result, an investigation was opened. Officer Andrews is on paid suspension."

The Internal Affairs Lieutenant said, "The deliberation is beginning." He gave the date, time, and he introduced every single person at the table.

"Back in 2015, the Las Vegas Police Department implemented body cameras on all police officer personnel. With body cameras, we can view a first-hand account of what happened. We use it as a tool to determine if an officer committed a violation or misconduct. If you look up at the TV monitor, you'll see what we could see that day."

I looked up at the monitor. I heard myself running, moving people out of the way. Kiarra, Kosby, and Stacey were standing there looking look like deer caught in headlights. They grabbed each other's hands in anticipation of what was to come. Grabbing Kiarra, I thrashed her as the crowd gathered around the terrible episode. It was awful seeing the terrified looks on their faces. Like a malfunctioning robot, I beat her. I beat her until I drew blood until her clothes draped her body like shredded rags. The beating was violent. Next, my partner came into the frame; he grabbed me, pulled me away from this woman.

The internal affairs Lieutenant said, "Now we will watch the body camera of his partner Officer Vernon Meadows. Again, they dimmed the lights, and we watched the TV monitor. My partner was talking to a concerned citizen about a problem when someone pointed out the commotion. He took off running, and from his point of view, you could see him pulling me off Kiarra.

"Man, stop, this isn't right, stop!" He insisted as he wrestled me away from her.

The Internal Affairs Lieutenant said, "We have one more to show. It's a video taken by a concerned citizen. They dimmed the lights to play the footage. From this view you could see the opposite; me running to Kiarra. With no warning, I threw punches. You could hear the same screaming that was on the other recordings, but this version shows something different, it shows that the encounter was unprovoked by the woman. The Internal Affairs Director tapped on his microphone.

"Officer Andrews, do you have any defense about what happened?"

"Yes, Lieutenant, we would like to call the precinct Psychiatrist Dr. Malone." My Union

Steward countered. The officer was instructed to get Dr. Malone. Dr. Malone entered and was shown to a seat where he was instructed to speak into the microphone. Dr. Malone cleared his throat.

"Officer Andrews is my patient. I have been treating him for acute insomnia. We started with a mild sleep aid Lunesta. Nothing seemed to work, so I put him on a stronger sleep aid. Halcion is a benzodiazepine which can be addictive; it's used to treat insomnia. Halcion is also 8.7 times more likely to be linked with violence than other drugs."

The Internal Affairs Lieutenant questioned. "Dr. Malone, is it standard operating procedure to give police officers medication that has side effects to make them violent?"

Dr. Malone said, "Officer Andrews has an exemplary record with the department. He was next in line for promotion to detective. He was exhausted and worried about his lack of sleep affecting his performance. We use all sleeping medication as a short-term cure. I was seeing Officer Andrews twice a week while he used the last prescription. I checked him for any side effects, including violence, and he passed. I told him I would not renew this prescription because of its addictive qualities."

The internal affairs lieutenant asked, "Dr. Malone did your patient talk to you about the victim Kiarra Maxwell?"

Dr. Malone replied, "legally, I am bound by doctor-patient confidentiality."

The internal affairs lieutenant said to the union steward, "You may question the witness."

"Thank you," said the Union Steward. "Dr. Malone you said that Halcion was 8.7 times more likely to cause a patient to be violent. Could you please explain to us what that means?"

Dr. Malone said, "It's not what you think mathematically; for example, it doesn't mean 8.7% out of 100. They compare medications used to treat the same ailments. And based on the studies, they come up with the numbers. There are a lot of variants in these studies because they test people with the medication, and some receive placebos. The mind is powerful, so even patients with placebos are sometimes cured. Also, some patients experience side effects by reading the pamphlet insert that comes with some medications. It's because of that a lot of pharmacies don't include the pamphlet when they fill a prescription. Some people Google side effects of medicines when there is no pamphlet to see what the side effects are. So technically that 8.7 was a comparison with all medications used for insomnia."

"Thank you, Dr. Malone." said the union steward.

Dr. Malone chimed in the with the internal affairs lieutenant.

"How can we find out what that 8.7 means in a common mathematical form like percentages?"

"Lieutenant, you could call the pharmaceutical company, and they can give you that calculation in percentage points."

"Thank you, Dr. Malone; you are dismissed."

"Officer Andrews, we want to inform you that this action has gone through your chain of command.

The Chief said, "Officer Andrews, it was difficult for me to have made a decision that was this detrimental to the department. You have placed the department in a very uncomfortable situation. We have prided ourselves on being one of the best departments in the United States. All our officers know they are wearing body cameras; you have been told to use force sparingly; we do not abuse people. We are not that kind of department. You will remain on paid suspension until we complete our investigation. Do you understand your rights, Officer Andrews?"

"Yes, sir," I said demurely.

The Chief said, "This meeting is adjourned."

Chapter Twenty-Nine

Kosby

I talked to my brother Chris on the phone.

"This has to be between you and me. I mean it. You can't tell Kiarra because she has litigation going with the city, and I don't want her to know what happened at a private hearing."

"No problem, Chris, blood first!"

"Derrick's excuse was he's on a medication where the side effect could evoke violence. It worked, too, because they were all set to terminate him, but they kept him on paid suspension to investigate his claim."

"Wow, he's smarter than I gave him credit for."

"Me too, sis. I was so angry. I broke a pen with my bare hands."

I laughed, "You haven't changed. No worries, my lips are sealed."

"All right, I'll talk to you soon."

"Okay, Chris, later."

I strolled over to Kiara's room and tapped on the door.

"Do you need anything? Are you thirsty? Want a little snack or something?"

"No, I'm good. I'm still full from dinner. Thank you so much. It was delicious."

"I'm glad you enjoyed it, Kiarra. I will wash the dishes. Let me know if you want anything, just yell."

I washed all the dishes and put them in the dishwasher. I was bored. I wanted to do my favorite thing, which was to get myself a manicure and a pedicure. Again, I walked up to Kiarra's room and knocked.

"Come in," she said.

"Hey, I'm leaving for a bit. Can I get you anything before I leave?"

"Yes, if you could just throw me in a bottle of water before you go, I'll be fine," she said.

"Sure, sweetie, no problem." I went to the refrigerator and got an ice-cold bottle of water. I took it in, gave it to her, and shut her door. I drove over to my nail shop and got my pedicure, which relaxed me. I hadn't permitted myself to think about Deion, but he was on my mind now. I got angry all over again, thinking about our argument. He was so selfish. He wouldn't even compromise with me until we came up with a permanent solution. My mom and dad were the king and queen of compromise. They genuinely loved each other. That's where I believed Deion and I were going, but no, he was still a selfish little boy who had to have it his way or no way. If he were waiting for me to give in, he'd be waiting for the rest of his life. It would be on with the next woman to deal with his selfishness because I didn't care. I wish he knew how much I didn't care; I wished his friends knew how much I didn't care, I wished his mama knew how much I didn't care, I wished his little niece knew how much I didn't care, because I don't care!

My manicurist took me over to the pedicure tub, filled it with hot water, added some blue crystals, and guided me to put my feet into the water. It was perfect. She took turns clipping my toenails, shaping them and putting them back into the water, all the while, my chair vibrated me into a relaxed state. Pedicures were great stress relievers. The manicurist rubbed my legs and feet with hot coals; it felt so good. This is what I called living. After she finished with the hot coals, she then massaged my legs with a thick lotion until they were nice and shiny, last she applied the polish making my feet summer ready, which was year-round in Las Vegas.

The manicurist did the same for my hands and applied the same polish used on my toes. She puts me under the heat lamp, and when my nails were all done, I paid for my service and gave her a tip.

Since it was still early, I rode over to the mall. It wasn't long before I found a pair of shoes, a dress, and a matching handbag. Between my nails and my outfit, I was ready for tomorrow. There was nothing like a little shopping therapy to get over a relationship gone south. It was still hard to believe after all the fun times we had, everything was wiped away after one argument. Feeling tired, I headed back home with my new stuff. I checked on Kiarra, who had climbed into bed. I grabbed myself a Lime-a-Rita to drink and help me wind down while I watched the news. Afterward, I washed my face really good, and added moisturizer to keep my skin supple, put my nightgown on and off to bed I went.

I felt so good today in my new outfit, with my nails done, makeup on, you couldn't tell me anything. I felt wonderful. Plus, I was coming to terms with me not needing a man in my life to validate me as a woman. Everything I had; I gave the glory to God. He was the only man I would ever need. He would never leave me; he always helped me make it through the day. Hallelujah! I was so happy I almost skipped to my car today. I turned on Deitrick Haddon's Glory and started singing on my ride home:

Oh You, you get the glory

For everything you've done for me.

Just as I got ready to turn into my parking space, I noticed Deion sitting in my spot in a chair from the building. I stopped singing, but Deitrick doesn't, he's still jamming. I slammed on the brakes, put my car in park, and hollered out the window, "Deion, do you realize I almost hit you."

"But you didn't, and you had your chance." He stood up, moved the chair, and I put my car in drive and eased into the parking space.

"What are you doing here this evening; I thought you broke up with me."

"Baby, you know I wouldn't break up with you. I was having a moment, a selfish moment. My mother told me when I was a young boy that I selfish. I apologize. I wanted you to come to my church so bad that I didn't listen to reason even when you came up with the perfect solution, but I still didn't want to hear it. Still, since we haven't talked, I realized I would go to any church in this world to be with you. I'd do whatever it took for you to take me back."

"Deion, I watched my parents for years, in all that time I noticed that they would both compromise when they didn't exactly agree on a situation. My dad, he always loved being around his friends, but he would always say well guys it's time for me to go, happy wife, happy life. That used to tickle me because it meant he was thinking about her. My mom was forever thinking about dad, too; she would ask us what we wanted for dinner, then she would choose something that would please dad because he would be home. The things he didn't like, she'd make them for us while he was flying. So, I have seen firsthand what it takes to make a relationship work for over 40 years. If you decide that I'm the lady you want in your life, then you need to learn to how to compromise. See, I not only saw my parents, who to this day love each other, but I saw other relationships. My friend Stacey, her dad, was like you; he was the most selfish man I'd ever known in my life. He would walk around the house, and he would tell his wife what to do when to clean, what to cook, he was a ruler. Her mother was a nervous wreck. He ended up cheating on her, and they got divorced. It was a slow process watching her get her independence back, but once she realized what she was worth, she became a wonderful mother. She never remarried because I think she was afraid of losing that independence. The moral of this story is I had already decided what I wanted in a relationship. My girls used to joke and call me a perfectionist.

'She'll never find a perfect man,' they joked. I never even tried to argue with them, because I knew there was no perfect man other than Jesus Christ that ever walked this earth. Yet I looked for a man that would respect me as a woman and an equal partner, not tell me what to do or give me ultimatums as you did. I saw all of that in you, but that day you were so unreasonable, it would be your way or no way. I felt like God had blessed me with being able to see your true nature. So, if you want me back, you must understand that just because you're the man doesn't mean you may tell me what to do when to do it, or how to do it. We have to agree to be friends first, partners, and eventually, lovers for me to be happy in our relationship."

"Kosby, I know you're right; I can remember when my mother and father were together, he was very demanding, and my mother always complied. I can't say that I know why they broke up. Still, I remember my mother buying all her children and herself tickets to the

United States. When we got here, we stayed with some distant relatives in a ghetto in Brooklyn, New York. Looking back at how abruptly my mother moved us away, I see she was unhappy with my father and his antics.

My mother quickly found work. She worked such hard and long hours. She was able to save up most of her money. When she felt comfortable with the amount of money she had saved, she moved us to Las Vegas. I never understood why she moved to Nevada because we had no relatives here. She knew Vegas was big on mobile homes and figured she'd saved enough to purchase one. It would've been about the same amount of space we had growing up in Australia. Much to her surprise, Las Vegas had beautiful homes. Even the ghetto looked gorgeous in our eyes, so she purchased a brand-new tiny house in North Las Vegas. The was an area referred to as the hood. Shoot, our family was so happy; we thought we were rich. I look back on those days, and I realized something we were right about being rich; we had a mother that loved us, and friends in our neighborhood. We enjoyed playing. We would all walk to school together, come home, and do our homework. We always had dinner together at the table. I thought we were just like one of those old TV shows. It wasn't until one day I was at church this man kept calling us underprivileged. I didn't understand the word until I went home and asked my mother what it meant. She told me, and I said that man must have us mixed up with somebody else, and she laughed.

"Yes, because he probably lived in a different world and didn't understand the happiness of family," she told me.

I never forgot it; that's when I knew life wasn't about material things. It wasn't about things of the flesh, but it was about the love of God and all the blessings he bestowed on us each day. Kosby, if you forgive me, I promise to remember everything you told me and my own upbringing. I want to treat you like the queen you were born to be."

"Of course, I forgive you, Deion." Deion cupped his hands around my face. He kissed me delicately, allowing our foreheads to connect in thought.

"Now can we leave this parking garage," I said, and we laughed.

Chapter Thirty

Deion

I know my girl loved Deitrick Haddon because she was singing his song 'Glory' when she almost ran me over. I chuckled. It was my fault though I was so determined to speak with her, I pulled up a chair and sat in her parking space until she got home. I heard her singing Deitrick on blast singing every word with him, and I found out not only can she carry a tune, but she had a beautiful voice. I hadn't realized that she was such a big fan of Deitrick. Once I went home, I checked the computer for his concert schedule. I noticed his next scheduled performance was December 3rd at Alabama State University in Montgomery, Alabama. I grabbed my phone book to look up a friend, and sure enough, he lived in Montgomery, Alabama, so I called him. I told him how much my girlfriend loved Deitrick Haddon. He said he had a couple of extra tickets because he thought some friends would join him and his wife, but they backed out.

"Man, I'll give you these two tickets for free if you can make the trip."

"It's a date, my brother I'm glad to have

time to see you it's been a long time, and I'll take us all out to dinner before the concert."

"Awe brother, we can't go. It's the in-law's anniversary, so we will have dinner with them. It's the thought that counts, I'll send you the two tickets in the mail. I'll see you at the concert, man, because we'll be sitting next to each other." Gary said. I thanked Gary after making sure he had my correct address and hung up. My phone rang.

"Did I catch you at a good time?" Kosby asked.

"Yeah, perfect," I replied.

"Good because I have something to ask you, are you working tomorrow?"

"No, can you believe it. I have a day off."

"Well, you know it's Thanksgiving; do you already have plans?"

"No, I don't I thought I'd just take the day to chill and watch the game."

"I'd like to invite you over to my parents' house; we always do a big Thanksgiving dinner. Mom invites everybody she knows, and most of the family members. You'll have a good time with the men. You can watch the game, drink a beer, and enjoy yourself. Then we'll have a nice dinner, are you interested?"

"Yes, I'd love to go spend the holiday with you and your family. What time should I be ready?"

"My mother likes to make an early dinner,

around 2:00 p.m. I figured we could get over there around noon so I could help her in the kitchen."

"Okay, sweetie, I'll be down to pick you up about what 11:30?"

"11:30 would be perfect. I love you," she said.

"Until tomorrow. Sweet dreams, hopefully about me. I love you more."

We both hung up the phone. I was excited to spend the day with Kosby that call made me smile.

I checked my watch, it was 6:30 p.m. I had enough time to make it. I locked my door jumped in my car, and drove as fast as I could without breaking the speeding limit to my barbershop because I wanted to look my best. I arrived at the barbershop in record time. I ran in, and they were cleaning up.

"John, do you have enough time to edge me up?"

"Yeah, man, come on and have a seat. I sat in the chair while he cleaned up my face. John took my beard down to a five o'clock shadow. My hair grows so fast he trimmed the top, which I wear longer because I loved the texture of my hair.

"Thanks, John," I said as I gave him his fee and a tip.

I strolled back to my car, happy that Kosby called me early enough to get my hair done before going over her parents' house. I glanced in one of the stores; a blue shirt captured my attention because it was the same shade of blue as my eyes. I went into the store and bought it in my size. I was excited because this shirt would make my eyes pop. I would be so fresh.

On my way home, I stopped at a fast-food restaurant to order a bite to eat; I wasn't in the mood to cook tonight. I got home ate my food, drank my coke, and listened to some music until I nodded off, hoping to dream of Kosby.

Chapter Thirty-One
Kosby

I got up early, took my shower, and washed my hair. My hair needed time to air dry before Deion picked me up for Thanksgiving dinner. I dried off with a fluffy gray bath size towel after going through my regimen of lotions and doing my hair. I put on a fluffy robe and headed to the kitchen. I inserted a K-cup of cappuccino in my Keurig and waited for the delicious brew to fall into my cup. I sat down to drink my cappuccino, had a few grapes with half an orange so I wouldn't be starving when I got to my parents' house. Kiarra hobbled out her room. I invited her to eat breakfast with me.

"Do you want some grapes and the other half of this orange, or would you prefer a more substantial breakfast?"

"I'll take the grapes and the other half of the orange with a cup of hot chocolate, please."

I washed more grapes, got the other half of the orange, and stuck a K-cup of hot chocolate in the Keurig. Once I prepared everything, I sat back down with her.

"How is the litigation going against the City of Las Vegas?" I asked.

"My lawyer and I met with City officials. They offered me 100 grand, but my lawyer turned it down. He said that wouldn't even cover the medical bills. So, they came back with an offer of 150 grand, again my lawyer turned that down and said, that wouldn't cover my medical bills or my lawyer fees. So, they said they would have to talk with the City Council and the financial department to see if they could make another offer, or it would have to go to court. That ended the negotiations, and we left."

"Wow, I bet you were ready to accept the hundred thousand, weren't you?"

"Yes, I sure was ready to agree, because that was more money than I could ever imagine having at one time. But Chris recommended this lawyer to me, and he said he's the best, so I will do whatever my lawyer feels inclined to do."

"Girl, I don't blame you. Those are big sums of money, but believe me, he'll make them sweat, and your next quote will be closer to his liking. I'm telling you my brother is the bomb he always gives good advice. You'll be buying a house of your very own, paid for when your lawyer is finished negotiating."

"Kosby girl, you always keep me encouraged. I was feeling down like they'd say we're sorry, but we will go to court, and I'd end up even with less money than 100k. I tell you I've been sweating bullets."

"Don't worry, give it to God and let it go,

walk in faith, and whatever happens is the blessing that our Heavenly Father has blessed you with."

"Yeah, I've been reading my Bible, I prayed, I'm walking in faith I hope that Derrick gets whatever punishment the good Lord deems acceptable. I've looked at the literature on police officers; they have killed so many Black people, yet they get off and keep their jobs. Here he may get one little black spot on his record, get to keep his job, and continue to harass people. I wouldn't be the least bit surprised."

"You know things on this earth are often not fair. There's a passage in the Bible that said, 'Woe to those who call evil good and good evil, who put darkness for light and light for darkness, who put bitter for sweet and sweet for bitter.' It only proves that we must be vigilant in following our Lord because the day of reckoning is coming."

"Wow, that's deep," Kiarra said.

I loaded the dishwasher.

"I will get dressed, 11:30 a.m. will be here before you know it."

"Yeah, you're right," exclaimed Kiarra.

I went to my room, sat down at the dressing table, and applied my make-up. Using a light hand, I went for a natural face because it was daytime. A lot of the time, I prefer a nude lip, but I want to match everything up today, so I use a matte MAC lipstick named Sin, it's wine-colored, the perfect complement to my nails and top. My top was a beautiful wine color with silver grommets accenting it. I chose a silver Michael Kors charm bracelet for my left arm and a group of silver bangles for my right arm. No necklace but bold sterling silver hoops. I grabbed my worn-out toothbrush, added a bit of styling gel, and laid down my baby hair. I finished my ensemble with a pair of black jeans and black suede heels. I grabbed a black tote bag, put a t-shirt and house shoes inside. I didn't want to mess up my shirt cooking or standing in heels. I sat the tote bag and my Michael Kors bag at the front door, so I would be ready when Deion came by. I walked over to Kiarra's room, knocked on the door. She told me to come in.

"Hey, just checking to see if you're almost ready?"

"Yes, I've done the best I can do."

I looked at her, and she was gorgeous. "Oh, my you look stunning my friend, your face has healed up so nicely, from a few weeks ago you look like a different person."

"Thank you, Kosby, because they said that the one black eye was fractured, and they could do nothing about it. I thought I would have a permanent crazy looking face, so even though that bones fractured underneath, it doesn't show. When all the bumps, bruises, and scratches went away, I started to feel more and more like myself. With each step, I felt better.

When they took the cast off my fractured foot and gave me a booted foot, I was ecstatic because I could take that thing off at night. Now, I'm only dealing with one hard cast."

"I know it's amazing. I can't tell by your face that anything has happened. You look so beautiful. I'm sure that you can party and have a wonderful time at my parents' house today for Thanksgiving, it won't be long before everything is back to normal."

"I know when I get all of this litigation completed, I can get back to my normal life. I talked to my boss, and since I'm able to maneuver around with the boot and the crutches, he said I can come back to work, so I'll be going back to work on Monday even though my lease is up on my apartment. I have to go on and pay rent because all my stuff is still in there."

"That must be the hardest part of this whole tragedy because everybody likes to have their independence, but I have enjoyed having you with me. I think I'll be kind of sad when you leave."

"Kosby, you are absolutely the best friend anyone could ever have."

I smiled at her then the doorbell rang, I told her,

"That's Deion. He's right on time."

"Okay, I'm coming," she says.

I opened the door, and there he stood. I

couldn't believe this handsome man belonged to me.

"Hey, baby," I say.

"Hey, you ready?"

"Yes, we're ready."

"I can go get the car and pull it around and make it easier on Kiarra."

"I thought I'd drive because your SUV is too high for her to climb into my little car is a lot easier for her to maneuver, is that okay with you?" I asked.

"Great, I finally get the luxury of being chauffeured around."

"You know you're welcome to drive my car if you want to."

"No, no, no," he replied. "I'm looking forward to being chauffeured, which means I can drink as much beer as I want too."

"Oh yeah now I get it, I'm the designated driver."

Kiarra joined us, I set the alarm, and we proceeded to the elevator. We went down to the parking level. Deion waited with Kiarra while I pulled the car around. Shocked to find a parking place right in front of my parents' home, I pulled right in.

We piled into the house, and everyone spoke to everyone. Deion and Kiarra sat on the love seat that faced the television. I could tell Deion was happy because he was ready to watch the game. I took my stuff and moved on to the kitchen where I sat my things down as I watched my aunt and my mom, and my cousin cooking dinner. The scent was amazing. I smiled at my mom and spoke to everyone.

"Okay, what do you want me to do.

My mom gave me instructions, and I went into the bedroom and changed my shirt, put on my house shoes, went into the bathroom, and washed my hands. I joined the ladies in the kitchen, and I began doing everything my mother instructed me to do.

I was used to this from the time I was a teenager. I worked with my mother, not only on holidays but many days to prepare for dinner. I appreciated all of that now because I knew how to make so many great dishes. It was a good experience for me to learn how to cook when I was finally on my own. I thought about all the days I didn't want to eat any fast food. I would always grocery shop the way my mother taught me. I would cook a full dinner usually the second night I would eat leftovers. But with Kiarra staying with me, we could knock off a meal, and the next day the, other person would cook. I grabbed a Heineken and took it out to Deion.

"Kiarra, would you like something to drink?" I asked.

"Yes, a Coke, please."

I grabbed a nice cold Coke and gave it to her. I returned to my station in the kitchen to finish what my mother asked of me; then, another task would appear. I knew this would go on most of the afternoon. But it was fun. I always loved hearing my mom and aunt talk; they were hilarious, my cousin, and I were cracking up. We laughed so hard at one point nobody was getting any work done. So, we shut up for a minute and got back to work, my cousin told me about her new boyfriend.

I said, "Awe, did you bring him?"

"No, he couldn't come. He had to go to his parents' home. They live out of state," she said. My cousin was a junior at UNLV.

As we finished up the food, I could hear more guests arriving. I knew my job was to set the table, but when I saw all the people, I knew we wouldn't fit. I informed my mom, who got my dad to put the leaf in the table. They also carried in another table; mom put a tablecloth on it while dad got the chairs. I put table settings at every seat. Mom had beautiful, serving dishes. She put out collard greens. Herb roasted turkey and cornbread stuffing, giblet gravy, mashed potatoes, cranberry sauce, spiral glazed baked ham, oven-roasted corn on the cob, macaroni and cheese, broccoli casserole, yams, rolls and for dessert sweet potato pie, pecan pie, and peach cobbler. It was, indeed, a feast. We held hands, and my father said the blessing. Everyone began to dig in as my father carved the turkey with his electric knife. The food was delicious, the conversation stimulating, and everybody was stuffed.

While mom and Aunt Vera were watching the game with the family, my cousin and I cleared the tables, washed all the dishes, and put them away. My cousin joined the family while I took off the tablecloths, put them in the wash. I polished mom's table and put the centerpiece back in the middle. I got the swifter to clean the wood floors in the dining room. Dad came in gave me a big hug and a kiss on the cheek.

"Kosby, I love you, my princess. What a nice gift for your mom. But you've always been a perfectionist."

"Daddy, you think I'm a perfectionist?"

"Of course, you are. As a child, you never half did anything. If you couldn't do it, you would work at it and work some more until you could complete the task perfectly. Sweetheart, that's not a bad trait to have. Remember that not everyone is a perfectionist like you, so when others fall short of your standards, don't judge them. Many people go through life, believing they are mediocre at best. Not my business. You and Deion are a great couple, he is inquisitive and wants to know how everything works; he was the best co-pilot I ever had the pleasure of working with daily. Because he has a lot of the same personal ethics that you have, he earned the opportunity to fly a plane. I shouldn't say this, but almost every cute young flight attendant tried to hook up with him, but they all fell short of what he was looking for in a woman. He's a good Christian and would not settle for anything less than a woman with his values. I was proud to see you with him; it let me know that you had embraced the ethics mom, and I tried so hard to instill in you. You and Chris are such a joy to us. The Bible said, 'Train up a child in the way he should go, and when he was old, he would not depart from it.' I give all the glory to God."

Chapter Thirty-Two

Derrick

I have been clean and sober for six weeks now. They called me back for my second hearing at the Las Vegas Police Department. I was nervous and a little shaky because I just couldn't come to grips with the fact that today I might lose my job.

It seemed like Deja vu, sitting in the same spot with my union steward waiting to be summoned, to address management. An officer came out told my union steward and me to come in and show us where to sit. This time the room was already full, my Police Sergeant, my Lieutenant, the Lieutenant of Internal Affairs, the Commander, the Deputy Chief of Police, and the Chief of Police were already seated. The internal affairs lieutenant cites the day the time and the hour of this meeting.

"Officer Andrews, today, we are here to inform you of the decision we've come up with regarding your employment with the City of Las Vegas Police Department. We took a lot of time to investigate the medication that you were on and your exemplary record as an officer. The behavior you showed the day you attacked a Las

Vegas citizen was deemed too violent to keep you on the job. Your pay will continue through today; tomorrow marks your official termination. To inform you, the City Attorney is also pressing charges against you. Officer Stone, please let the summons be served." Officer Stone walked to the door and let the summons server enter the hearing room. He walked to me and handed me a warrant for court. He then turned and left the hearing room.

The Internal Affairs Lieutenant said. "You have 60 days to appeal this decision. Do you understand your rights, Officer Andrews?"

"Yes, Lieutenant."

The Lieutenant said. "This meeting is adjourned."

Once we were out in the hall, my Union Steward pulled me to the side.

"I will appeal your case. Now it will depend on what happens to you in criminal court. If you win, you'll likely get your job back; if you lose, they will uphold your dismissal, do you understand?"

"Yes, I understand. Can you recommend a good attorney?" I asked, feeling slightly hopeful.

"I can recommend several great attorneys for you; I'll call you in a couple of hours with that information."

I shook his hand, and we both went our separate ways. I couldn't remember ever being this upset in my entire life. I wanted to drink, but I knew that I'd been clean and sober for six weeks. I would not let this situation ruin that. In the meantime, I would figure out a way to start my own business because I obviously wouldn't be working for the City.

My biggest fear was dealing with this criminal case. If found guilty, I would have to go to jail. I couldn't go to jail with all those criminals I put away.

Chapter Thirty-Three

Kiarra

I walked out of the meeting with my lawyer on cloud nine, today the big boot, the cast, and the crutches couldn't stop me from jumping for joy. The City of Las Vegas awarded me four hundred and fifty thousand dollars. I had to sign a non-disclosure statement, no problem. Kosby knew from day one I would get paid! She said I could buy me a house in cash and never worry about paying a mortgage or rent again.

I was thrilled, but also at the expense of never wanting to be in a relationship again. I didn't need therapy to know I would need to trust someone much less love them. No, I had no desire ever to go there again. I always wanted a beautiful home, but I didn't need to get my brains knocked out to receive it. I would buy myself a brand-new house, pick out the materials and new furniture. I might join Kosby's church, start reading my Bible, become a volunteer to usher, or be a missionary or something. I might even learn to love myself again.

I took a Lyft to Kosby's condo and cooked us a nice dinner. Spaghetti with meat sauce, the garlic bread ready to go in the oven once she got home. I made some sweet iced tea and poured myself a glass while I waited for her to come back.

I had the food on a very low simmer. I looked at new housing developments on the computer.

I heard Kosby coming in, so I got up, grabbed my crutches, and made my way back to the kitchen. Washed my hands, put the garlic bread in the oven.

"Hey, Kiarra, how did the day go? I'm interested in finding out what happened."

"It went better than I ever thought it would. I have a non-disclosure agreement, so I'm not able to tell anybody about Derrick or about the amount of money that I will receive. But Kosby, you are my very best friend in the world, and without you, I wouldn't have even known what to do, so please promise please not to ever divulge this."

"Girl, you know I would never divulge anything you told me."

"I got four hundred and fifty thousand dollars plus the city of Las Vegas will pay my lawyer's fees."

"Shut the front door. I am so happy for you. I told you you'd be able to get a house and pay for it."

I smiled. "Kosby, all I could think was you were right. I'm still not finished going to court.

They served me with a subpoena to testify against Derrick in a criminal case; my lawyer is also suing him in a civil case. I'm not sure how long it will take to get rid of that man."

I pulled the garlic bread out of the oven; It was perfect. I fixed two plates for Kosby and me. Kosby washed her hands we sit at the counter, said our prayers, and ate.

"This is delicious, Kiarra; I didn't realize I was so hungry. Girl, this garlic bread is so good, now I have to go to the gym, to work this meal off," Kosby joked.

"Kosby, would you mind taking me house hunting this weekend?"

"I'd love to. I always enjoyed looking at the model homes to get decorating tips. Deion is flying this weekend, so that would be perfect. Next weekend he is taking me to Montgomery, Alabama."

"That's nice, does he have family there or something?" I inquired.

"No, he doesn't have family there. It seems like a weird place to take our first vacation together, but he invited me, so I'm all in," she said.

"Did he go to school there; I don't get it?" I asked.

"No, he graduated from the Air Force Academy in Colorado Springs."

"Well whatever he has planned. I'm sure you'll enjoy it."

"I'm sure I will, I enjoyed being with Deion, even when we stay home to watch movies. We can house hunt Saturday morning; those places usually open up at 9 or 10 a.m. so let's leave about 9:30 a.m."

"Okay, it's a date." I grinned, showing all my pearly whites.

Kosby and I went to about five or six model homes sites. I was shocked at how expensive the new homes were. Most of the houses were two stories, and they were enormous; I didn't feel I needed a home that size. I asked the salesperson if they had any ranch-style homes. They all explained that it cost more money to build a smaller house on a larger lot because it took up more space. To me, that was unbelievable. They were all so greedy. All I wanted was a small one-story house with a decent-size backyard. I was also hoping to get a swimming pool. The land they gave you was itty-bitty. I was frustrated, but thank goodness Kosby suggested we go to Henderson to look.

We went to a model home community. They had a nice mixture of two-story and one-story houses. I looked at all the one-story homes, and oh my goodness. They had everything I wanted from the open floor plan, three bedrooms, a large master bedroom with master bath, and a jacuzzi tub. Not to mention all the trimmings a person desired, but the French door and the pool sold me. Outside were beautiful travertine pavers. The pool had beautiful blue water with a rock garden and waterfall on one side.

"Kosby, this is it. This is the house I want."

"Well, let's go inside to see if you can have you one built."

We went inside and spoke to the sales agent.

"This particular community is sold out, but we are selling the models. So, if you want this house, I think we can work out a deal. Come on into my office. When we get to the point of selling the model, you always get a better deal. This house could easily run you over four hundred thousand, but I'm sure I could talk my employer into letting you have it for three hundred and fifty thousand.

"She will give you three hundred and twenty thousand in cash for this model. You have her information call her and let her know if your employer will accept cash," Kosby offered.

"Okay, I will talk to them. Kiarra, I promise to get back to you ASAP." We all shook hands and left. Before she started the car, she said,

"Give me your hands."

I did as he requested.

"Bow your head. God, please give Kiarra favor." She then let go of my hands while I rambled on and on about the house as she drove us home.

Once we were at Kosby's condo, I laid on my bed, looking at all the pictures on my phone I had taken of the house. I daydreamed about it until I fell asleep. My phone rang. It scared me it was so loud I woke up. I still had the phone in my hand, so I answered it. The sales agent told me the builder had a counteroffer, three hundred and thirty thousand, and I could keep all the furniture in the model. I immediately accepted.

"Can you come back tomorrow to complete the paperwork, and then we can set a date for closing."

"Yes, of course, I'll be there. Thanks again." I said.

I got up using my crutches I found Kosby watching television. I told her about the counteroffer.

"That is fantastic; I was in love with its layout!"

"Me too!" I said.

EPILOGUE

Kosby and Deion are still in love. He visits one Sunday at her church, the next weekend he works. On the third weekend, Kosby attends his church the following weekend Deion works. It was a nice compromise. Let's pray; they come up with a permanent solution.

Kiarra purchased her new home. She got to take the boot off. She got the hard cast removed from her other foot, and it was replaced with a boot.

Derrick lost his criminal and civil case. He currently resides at Northern Nevada Correctional Center.

Stacey and Carl are expecting their first child, Kosby is looking forward to being a Godmother.

The End.

About the Author

Garnet (Hankins) Wells, a native of Denver Colorado, passed away on June 7, 2018, in Las Vegas, Nevada, shortly after completing her first novel Mesmerized.

Garnet, a graduate of East High School, thereafter, attended The University of Colorado Boulder, graduate school, earning her Master's Degree in Journalism. Garnet enjoyed working for the State of Colorado before relocating, in 1986, to Columbus, Ohio where she was employed with the City of Columbus before retiring from Anheuser Busch. Upon retirement, Garnet moved to Las Vegas in 2011 to enjoy her 'golden years with her husband.' She enjoyed spending time with her two daughters, four grandkids, and six great-grandkids.

Garnet Wells